THE COLT OF DESTINY

******

to Fred,
thank you for
giving us your truck.

MANUELA SCHNEIDER

Hope to meet you next
time.

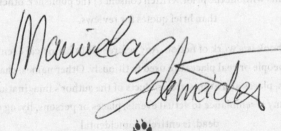

WOLFPACK
PUBLISHING
— EST 2015 —

WOLFPACK PUBLISHING
— EST 2013 —

Paperback Edition
Copyright © 2021 Manuela Schneider

Wolfpack Publishing
5130 S. Fort Apache Road 215-380
Las Vegas, NV 89148

wolfpackpublishing.com

Paperback ISBN 978-1-64734-745-1
eBook ISBN 978-1-64734-744-4

THE COLT OF DESTINY

******

CHAPTER ONE

***

ARIZONA TERRITORY 1882

The Peacemaker lay lightly in his hand. He had always preferred six-shooters to rifles and was glad he'd found this fine gun. Or should he say, the Colt had found him?

Well, he remembered the day when he met that young soldier five years ago. The feller complained about being short of money and desired more than anything to run away and start a new life with his sweetheart. She was a woman of easy morals, as Johnny knew from firsthand experience. Dreaming of playing husband and wife, the lovesick fool sold him the six-shooter in a rush, far below the price he could have obtained for it.

The dang greenhorn wasn't worthy of a fine weapon like this, nor could he handle a woman of her trade, Johnny thought. Smirking, Johnny recalled how the lad in his stained uniform had whined about bad luck always following him.

Johnny couldn't say such a thing. He always made sure "lady luck" stayed with him. He believed that a man has to create his fortune like a blacksmith forged a hot piece of iron. Strength, willpower, and backbone were required. Whenever Johnny's luck faded, he helped it back on its feet.

He was a ruthless desperado and didn't mind dodging the law. In more than one encounter, he had proven his lack of respect for the law dogs of the territory. The outlaw was known for constantly bragging that he didn't fear even the devil himself. Most likely he didn't know any better.

He was self-confident to the point of foolishness. Johnny was one of the deadliest gun hands along the frontier and the leader of a gang called the Cowboys. They rode the brand loyally, so Johnny was never short of a supportive gun or money, which he earned from gambling or selling stolen cattle on both sides of the border.

The gunslinger was a regular guest in the territory's bodegas and houses of ill repute. But lately he had too much of a taste for the opium tents and the petite lotus flowers who would serve any man's need.

Johnny had been in the Hoptown neighborhood, as the Chinese part of Tombstone was nicknamed, far too often and had developed an addiction to the opium drug faster than he would have thought possible. But he didn't mind as he was convinced that nothing and no one could harm him.

He wasn't dumb. He just didn't fear the consequences of the sins he committed. He considered his soul as lost anyway, and he had no intention of changing that. His soul had died the day he watched his father blow his brains out. Johnny was fifteen then. People said it had been an accident. Whether accidental or not, the circumstances didn't erase the image that was branded onto his subconscious, leaving him traumatized.

The memory of his dying father with his brains splattered across the prairie haunted him almost every night.

He drowned it with bottled courage and was often soaked. Yet the more he drank, the more it required, and soon an entire bottle of family disturbance was necessary to chase away the ghosts from the past.

***

So now here he was, cleaning his favorite Colt while all these unwanted memories thronged his mind. For two days in a row the gunslinger and his friends had been gambling in a town close to the border of old Mexico. Although one of his poker partners was a close friend, Johnny had been merciless as he emptied the feller's pockets. He was supposed to meet the unlucky chap for a game tomorrow. Johnny was sure the tenderfoot would have calmed down by the time they met again. However, he was not foolish enough to believe that a friendship might not end in an instant. Such was life—one man's gain was another's loss, right?

On impulse, the tired gunslinger had decided to camp there at Turkey Creek the previous night and wait at this spot for the other gang members to join him the following day. Lately, it was safer for the cowboys not to ride close to the silver boom towns. Too much trouble was boiling, and several of the gang had been sent to Boot Hill.

The dang law dogs are hunting us down on a cruel vendetta as if we was rabbits to chase. Johnny didn't care much for other people's lives, but he wasn't willing to throw his own away.

He still battled a severe hangover in the aftermath of their poker spree. Walking around his campsite, his legs felt as if they would give way beneath him. He sat on the ground next to shallow Turkey Creek and leaned against a tree. *There, that was much more comfortable.* His hands shook as he cleaned his Colt. It was hard for him to re-load the bullets without dropping them.

As usual, when working with the Peacemaker, he felt a numbness and tingling in the hand that held it. The sensation always spread from the tips of his fingers and soon turned his entire hand numb and cold.

Johnny had no idea why, but it happened every time he held the weapon with its blue metal barrel. He blamed the excessive alcohol abuse. But luckily his ability to shoot with deadly aim had never failed him. He had developed into a sure shot over the past years.

He sat and admired the blueish metal of the six-shooter in his hand. An engraved registration number was visible on the barrel. The small number indicated this was one of the first army Colts produced around 1876— the engraving read "222." He had seen it countless times, yet today it looked blurry, hard to read.

Johnny blinked, but the numbers looked more like a crooked row of sixes than twos. *Strange*, he thought. As he blinked again, he saw them clearly. The engraving read "666."

"My, oh my, I think I have to watch the amount of corn juice I put in my gut. I cannot afford to lose my aiming ability, or I'll be a dead man," he mumbled while he finished loading his gun.

His head ached from the hangover, and he grimaced from the stabbing pain behind his temple. He felt queasy, and he heaved as if to throw up, but he'd hardly eaten the past twenty-four hours and nothing came up. The headache grew worse minute by minute, driving him to distraction. He rubbed his temple with his left hand, squeezing his eyes shut. When he opened them again, he saw a dark shadow standing close to him between the mesquite bushes. Johnny intended to jump to his feet as he didn't recognize the stranger, but his legs wouldn't work right.

"Who are you?" he barked angrily at the other man.

The stranger didn't answer. He wore a black hat with a wide rim that threw a shadow over his face. Johnny got mad when the stranger remained silent, and he brought up his gun. Before he could aim at the unknown man, a lance of pain behind his temple made him feel as if a nail were being driven into his skull. He groaned and clutched his head.

His vision grew blurry as he stared at the gun in his hand. He watched it rise, the barrel shaking. His hand felt icy, numb, detached, as if it wasn't his own.

Johnny intended to shoot the figure in black clothes. It would have been a sure shot, only a few yards from him. Instead, he saw his hand turning the barrel toward his own skull.

"Now wait a minute. What in the Sam Hill is happening here?"

The man smiled at him. He lifted his head and Johnny finally saw the stranger's face. His eyes were black as coal. He didn't speak but stood and watched. Johnny experienced a new emotion—fear. His eyes widened, and his heart pounded in his chest. Now his hands shook not because of the hangover, but from terror of the stranger who controlled his movement.

He struggled to use his other hand to aim the gun at the man standing across from him, but couldn't move a muscle except his eyes. A full-throated chuckle brought his attention back to the stranger, as Johnny realized his enemy was enjoying his predicament. Motionless and unspeaking, his features hidden by his hat, the stranger laughed scornfully.

Drops of sweat rolled down Johnny's face as he confronted his demise. "Who are you?" He felt the cold metal of the muzzle press against his temple, as he willed any muscle to move, to get him out of this death-trap.

A gunshot ripped through the peaceful afternoon air, and a crow flew away, complaining that its bath in the shallow creek had been disturbed. Next to the water a man sat on the ground, leaning against a tree, not moving. His legs were sprawled out in front of him.

A small bleeding wound at his temple and the blood on the tree bark were the first things a German teamster saw when he approached the body. He noticed the shape from the seat of his lumber wagon and signaled the horses to stop next to the trail.

Suicide? Must be, but if that were the case, the poor soul should be holding the weapon, shouldn't he?

He drove his team of draft horses into town and informed the law dog about finding the body of a man out at Turkey Creek.

The sheriff took the old doctor to the corpse. The physician completed the death certificate in his office at home later that evening. It read:

Cause of death—suicide by self-inflicted gunshot wound to the temple.

Deceased's identity—John Peters Ringo, known as Johnny Ringo.

Date of death—July 13th, 1882.

An additional line written on the death certificate stated that the weapon Johnny Ringo used to commit suicide was not found nearby.

Ringo's body wasn't brought back into town but buried there by Turkey Creek next to the tree where he was found.

The blued Colt was gone.

CHAPTER TWO

***

NEW MEXICO 1885

She stood at the kitchen window enjoying the smell of freshly baked rolls when her attractive husband walked into the kitchen and reached for the warm baked goods. He pretended to steal a roll.

She turned around with her index finger raised, her face showing the stern expression of a mother who was about to scold her child.

"Don't you dare touch those bread rolls, John Carson. These are for our dinner with my father."

His face looked like a little boy who had been caught with his hand in the cookie jar. He rolled his eyes and put his hands behind his back, pretending he didn't want any of the yummy-smelling rolls. She laughed at his antics, never able to resist his sparkling, blue eyes. "Alright, but only one, and then you are out of this kitchen of mine."

He smiled at her like a cheeky boy. That smile had captured her heart from the very first moment she had seen him at the army fort. At that time, her father had been the ranking officer, but that was before he gave up his military career and joined a mining operation.

John Carson stepped forward, embraced his wife, and kissed her tenderly on the cheek. Then he grabbed one of the warm rolls and turned toward the door. "I'll be outside at the corral, training that new horse."

"Be careful, my love."

"Yes ma'am." He saluted her jokingly and left the kitchen. Elizabeth watched from the kitchen window as her husband walked over to the horse corral. His stride was self-confident, and his lean body packed with muscles. He was the perfect picture of a hardworking, yet handsome rancher. Elizabeth smiled. Yes, John Carson was a good man, and he was not hard to look at, either.

Despite being madly in love with him, their relationship had been rocky at the beginning. Her father had made things difficult for the two lovebirds at the start. He was a well-respected, retired Army colonel with strict moral standards and even stricter rules when it came to his only child, Elizabeth. He expected the same kind of discipline from her that he did from his soldiers.

The early death of Elizabeth's mother had turned colonel Breckenridge into a controlling man. When he left the army, he ensured that Elizabeth remained with him for a few months, despite her being more than ready to start her own family with the man she had fallen in love with. Her father kept a close eye on her like a hawk, and it was obvious to everybody around them that he feared losing her just as he had lost his late wife. Respecting his love for her, Elizabeth never blamed him for his exaggerated urge to act as her protector.

But sometimes he behaved over-possessively, which was uncomfortable and even embarrassing for her. For a while, she feared it would chase John away.

Even at the beginning of their marriage Miles Brecken-ridge didn't hide his many doubts about John Carson. All those years in the Army had trained his instincts well, and he couldn't completely trust John. But finally, his daughter convinced the stubborn old colonel that John Carson was exactly the right man for her.

When they fell for each other, John had been hired as a wrangler at the military fort. He had invested much patience and time in convincing his future father-in-law that he was both hardworking and worthy to be his son-in-law.

In the end Miles Breckenridge gave the two lovebirds his blessing. During the following three years John Carson not only proved that he was the right man for Elizabeth Breckenridge but also was able to build a successful cattle ranch. However, Colonel Breckenridge could never en-tirely rid himself of his doubts about his son-in-law. The former army officer couldn't name what it was that still troubled him about the young feller. Especially since so far, the marriage had been a stable one, full of affection. He could see his daughter Elizabeth treasured and admired her husband, and she still had the special glow of a loving woman on her face. Yet his gut instinct told him that there was something about John Carson that didn't seem right. Those who knew the colonel well enough, read it in his serious expression and the frown he wore whenever people spoke about his son-in-law.

Elizabeth had her own thoughts about their marriage. She was aware that the love between them wasn't one of those burning flames of desire described in romantic novels. In the books often read by the soldiers of the army outpost, love was described as more passionate than she and John had. Elizabeth felt her cheeks blushing when she thought about the peeks she had snuck into those books.

The beautiful woman felt secure and happy in her relationship with John Carson, and she wanted nothing else, but lately it seemed as if he concentrated on their cattle operation. She couldn't help but wonder if the passion for their ranch had started to replace the possibility of a more intense kind of love and desire for her. With a frown she watched him walking over to the corral where the new stallion awaited, ears laid back. Elizabeth asked herself if the affection that she shared with John was as good as it ever got. From time to time, she caught herself fantasizing about being daringly seduced by her husband. But whenever that kind of thought arose, she shook her head and laughed at herself.

She wiped her hands at her apron. "You should be happy, girl. After all, we earn enough to afford a comfortable life in our beautiful ranch house. You can be proud of your man," she said into the empty kitchen. Despite the fact, that her father, Miles Breckenridge, was quite wealthy, John had never accepted money from his father-in-law. He was a proud man.

Sadly, Elizabeth didn't know anything about John's family or his life before they met. He had never spoken about it, and she didn't push him to. All she knew about him was that he grew up on a farm. Sometimes she regretted that they weren't in touch with his family. Most likely she would have enjoyed getting to know his mother because she missed her own very dearly. But thanks to his secrecy about his relatives, they were only in touch with her father. Elizabeth's eyes grew misty whenever she thought about it. She didn't want to admit it, but her life was lonely from time to time. She waited impatiently for him to return from his daily chores as she sat on the porch bench almost every evening. Yes, she would have loved to have his family around sometimes.

She could never have imagined that she would pay a high price for not knowing more about his past or where he came from.

CHAPTER THREE

***

THE HAPPY DAYS OF JOHN AND ELIZABETH CARSON

He rode slowly, lost in thought and asking himself over and
over again how it would be—the very first meeting after
all these years. The last time he had seen John was that one
fateful night when his entire life had changed.

The lonely rider tried to analyze his feelings. *Do I
still feel the same kind of hate that kept me alive all these
years?* Immediately after his escape, hate had burned like
a steady flame in his subconscious. *What do I feel now?*
He listened to his heart.

The cowboy stopped his horse and gazed into the valley.
No, he was not consumed by the same old fury. Instead,
controlled anger had replaced the burning hate. He felt
relentless determination to change the destiny that had
treated him so cruelly.

From his youth onward, he had always loathed injustice
and had not been at all prepared when he encountered it
within his own family. Nathanial would pay him back. It
wasn't so much about justice anymore as it was his desire

to resume his own life. But first he would find a place to sleep for the night. He led his horse toward the small town below in the valley.

***

The couple expected Elizabeth's father, Colonel Breckenridge, at their ranch for dinner at sundown. It was only a short ride from town to their cozy log cabin, and as usual, Breckenridge was on time. He could not give up his military discipline, although he was now a successful businessman. Despite the fact that he had exchanged his uniform for well-tailored suits, he still carried the bearing of a strict officer.

"Good evening, John. How are you getting along with that new stallion?" Miles Breckenridge took off his hat and placed it on the hook next to the door while greeting his son-in-law in a friendly manner.

"Great, Miles. But I have to admit it'll take a while before I'll be able to ride him. That stallion is as stubborn as an old mule."

Colonel Breckenridge joined in John's laughter and walked over to Elizabeth. He embraced her and gave her a tender little kiss on her forehead. "Hello, my beautiful butterfly."

"Hello, father. How's business at the mine?"

"Great, as usual. It was the best decision of my life to invest my saved-up money in that silver mine."

It was no secret to the folks in this area that Breckenridge earned a fortune every month since he left his position at the fort, but before her father could start a discussion about the mining operation, she planted her hands on her hips, and glared at both. "Well, boys, no talk about business while we're eating."

Her father rolled his eyes mockingly, but he obeyed her orders. "So, tell me, when will you two lovebirds make me a grandfather?"

"Father!" Elisabeth blushed. The question was not surprising, but she found it quite embarrassing, nevertheless. "Well, darling, you asked me to change the topic, didn't you?" Her father grinned back at her.

"I do believe that God will bless us with a child when he thinks the time is right, sir." John answered for his wife and smiled at her as her cheeks blushed a charming pink color.

"Your faith is strong my son," the colonel stated. John's facial expression turned serious. "My life hasn't always been this peaceful. My faith has kept me from despair and helped me not to forget my goals."

Breckenridge bent forward with a curious expression on his face. "John, thinking about it, I don't really know anything about your past or your family, and therefore it's kind of hard for me to judge how much hardship you really faced in life before you joined the Breckenridge Clan."

Elisabeth watched her husband closely. Just like countless times before, he quickly changed the subject when his family or his life before the wedding came up. Sometimes she wondered if he could be hiding something. During the entire three years they had been together, her husband had never spoken about his family or friends. She wished his parents had attended their wedding.

When she looked across the table, she witnessed a sudden cold glare in his blue eyes, and his wavy long hair couldn't hide the frown on his forehead. *Someday I may find out why he doesn't talk about his family,* she thought.

Conversation fell silent when she placed the bowls of steaming food on the table. Their dinner tasted delicious, and both men ate with huge appetites. Meatloaf and mashed potatoes were her father's favorite dishes, and it filled Elizabeth with joy to spoil him rotten with her cooking talents.

She knew her Dad longed for a real family life, and she was quite sure that he felt lonely in that beautiful townhome since his beloved wife had passed away.

After dinner, both men sat on the porch with a cup of hot coffee on a tray next to them. They spoke about the changes in meat prices as well as business at the silver mine. Elisabeth cut John's favorite pecan pie and offered both men a generous piece of it.

"Darling, you are definitely the best cook I know besides your late mother, may God rest her soul." Her father chewed happily, but the sadness still showed in his eyes whenever he spoke of Elizabeth's mom. His beloved wife had passed away way too young of smallpox, and he still missed her dearly.

Later that night as the young couple lay in their bed, they spoke about her father's wish to become a grandfather. Elizabeth had started to worry, wondering if something was wrong with her. Perhaps that was the reason she hadn't gotten pregnant yet. John was a tender lover and showed his respect for her with every touch. Elizabeth was scared that she would fail as a woman. *Maybe I should get some of those herbs that the native American women use.*

She had heard about such medicine when she lived in the fort with her father. A few Indians had a small camp just outside the palisades of the army post.

She considered riding to the fort and talking to some of the elder native women. She was quite sure they could help her. Unlike most white people, Elizabeth neither feared nor hated the Indians. She had always been fascinated by their culture and was interested to get to know more about it. Her father scolded her quite often whenever she tried to get in touch with them.

Colonel Breckenridge participated in the Apache wars and judged every American native as dangerous and hostile ever since. Whereas Elizabeth felt sympathy for them. She hated injustice and despite the fact that her father was a high-ranking officer and had faced some dangerous situations battling the Apache, she never understood why the destruction of the Indian culture was the chosen goal of the white settlers, the Army, and the government.

Elisabeth respected all human beings independent of their race or heritage. Wasn't it written in the Bible that every human on earth was a child of God and that they were all the same before God's throne?

Elizabeth had inherited the humble and friendly character of her beloved, late mother. She had a gentle and tolerant heart.

"Don't worry, darling. Soon we'll have a whole bunch of children running around. It just takes a little longer, but I trust in God." John interrupted her gloomy thoughts. He wanted to comfort her and held her in her arms. However, he kept his own thoughts about the topic to himself.

Elisabeth snuggled up close to him and after a few minutes, she heard his regular breathing and knew that he was fast asleep. She lay awake for a long time that night.

The following day John had to leave the ranch for a few days to help his neighbor gather his cattle since it was calf-branding season. The other ranch was approximately twenty-five miles farther down the river. Both livestock breeders helped each other when it was time to separate the calves from the mother cows.

Elisabeth packed everything necessary for John who would camp under the starlit sky for the duration of the cattle drive. He would stay until all the animals were rounded up.

John walked into the kitchen. He hugged and kissed her tenderly. "Thank you so much for readying everything for me, darling. I should be back home day after tomorrow, or at the latest in three days. Don't forget to lock the doors at night and keep that rifle close to you. You never know who is roaming around out there."

Elizabeth smiled at him. "Nobody will come here and steal me away from you, Mr. Carson."

They walked outside with their arms around each other, and Elizabeth watched him secure his saddlebags and mount the saddle. He turned his horse toward the gate, tipped his cowboy hat, and smiled at her in a last farewell. She waved at him and watched him disappear in a small cloud of dust.

Elisabeth walked back into the kitchen where a lot of work waited for her. The sun sent her warm rays of light through the small window. "Baking bread will have to wait until tomorrow," she mumbled. "First I have to go down to the creek and take care of the laundry."

CHAPTER FOUR

***

NATHANIAL

Nathanial rode slowly, choosing his route to the ranch carefully. He had slept in town and asked a few men at the local saloon where John Carson lived. By sheer accident he found out that John lived close to this settlement. It had taken years to track him down, but now Nathanial knew where to look for him.

Nate, as his few friends called him, had been a member of the cattle drive that delivered a small herd of horses to the nearby fort. During a conversation by the campfire, he spoke to one of the soldiers about horse breeding. The soldier told him about a man who had taken care of the fort's herd some time back. He mentioned that the wrangler had been the best so far, and that the horseman was called John Carson. The lad in uniform explained that the wrangler was a daredevil who had been lucky enough to marry the beautiful daughter of the former colonel of this army post.

"His job is available, and somebody has to tend our horses. In case you're interested I can put in a good word for you with our commanding officers."

Nathanial thanked the fellow but rejected the offer. He wanted to leave the fort as quickly as possible and hit the trail to John Carson's ranch. Once in town it hadn't been difficult to find where the property was located. It appeared that John's father-in-law was quite a well-known person in the area. And now Nathanial rode toward the cattle ranch that was supposed to be John's home.

For a brief moment Nate wondered about John's wife. *Does she have a clue as to what kind of man she married?* But his thoughts returned to the mission he was on. No one and nothing would stop him from taking the road he had chosen. This meeting would be crucial for his own future.

Nathanial stopped his horse and gazed down into the valley where the ranch lay nestled between lush fields and a creek. Everything was green, and colorful wildflowers added to the peaceful scenery. The day was warm, and bees buzzed in the air. Finally, he was close to John. He had waited nine long years for this moment...

***

It was early afternoon and Elizabeth carried the heavy basket with the wet laundry back to the house. She loved the smell of freshly washed clothes although it was hard work washing them in the cold creek.

When Elizabeth arrived at the steps to her porch, she saw a single rider coming toward the ranch. *Who that could be?* she wondered.

She put the basket down on the porch and waited with her fists resting on her slim hips. As the cowboy came closer to the house, she stepped back nervously toward the door. She had never seen this stranger. His expression was very serious. He sported a short beard which failed to hide his sensually curved lips.

When he pushed back his hat, she saw that he had green eyes with a slight hint of steely grey. His hair was wavy and long, past his shoulders. It was blond, and a few light wisps of grey added to his attractive looks.

Who in the world is he and what does he want out here? she wondered. She remembered John's advice to keep the rifle close by and looked at the door nervously. If only she hadn't laughed when her husband mentioned the Winchester. Right now, she wasn't in the mood to make fun of his worries. The Carsons weren't used to welcoming many visitors other than her father or their neighbor, and Elizabeth was concerned because her husband wasn't home.

The good-looking man tipped his cowboy hat and greeted her with a husky-sounding "Ma'am." Except for that, he didn't speak another word. Elizabeth straightened her shoulders and tried to look as confident as possible.

"What can I do for you, sir? Are you looking for someone?"

He didn't answer right away but watched her for a moment, then dismounted in one smooth movement. It caused the leather of his saddle to creak under his weight. When he stood next to his horse, Elizabeth realized the stranger was about two heads taller than she. He held the reins in his left hand and gently patted the neck of the sweaty horse with his other hand.

"I'm looking for John Carson. Folks in town told me that he lives on this ranch."

Elisabeth stood there dumbfounded for moment, surprised by the soothing sound and smooth timbre of his voice. She couldn't recall ever having heard such a pleasant, sultry male voice. To her own embarrassment, she felt herself blushing like a schoolgirl while he stood there patiently waiting for her answer.

Nathanial had heard that John was married, but he was definitely not prepared to meet such a fine woman. She was more than good-looking. Her features were delicate, her eyes sparkled like blue gemstones. Her long hair was tied back and caught the sunlight, reflecting it with a coppery shine. The soldiers in the fort hadn't exaggerated. Nathanial studied her and felt drawn to her lovely face. She was a real beauty, and her figure showed promising curves at the right spots

Elisabeth was so nervous she could barely stand still. "He is my husband, but he ain't home today. Can I pass him a message?" He didn't answer but kept staring at her. With each passing minute she felt more and more anxious.

"Your husband, hmm? I do have to talk with him. I'm a member of his family, if you want to call the Carson Clan a family, that is," he added with a sarcastic tone.

Elisabeth looked at him, speechless. Family? *Maybe it is something serious. It could be that he has news from my husband's parents. I shouldn't forget my good manners.* "Can I offer you a glass of cool lemonade? You look kind of thirsty, sir."

He smiled at her. "Yes Ma'am, I am indeed thirsty, and a glass of lemonade would be wonderful." She pointed to the bench on her porch and retreated into the house.

When she came back, she carried two glasses and a pitcher of lemonade on a tray. After thanking her he took a long sip. "That tastes really good and so refreshing. I have always considered my mother's lemonade to be the best in the West but this one sure beats hers." "Would you like some more?" She smiled warmly at him.

"Yes, please." He held his empty glass toward her. His hands looked strong, but his fingers were slender. A drop of lemonade rolled down the glass and across his tanned thumb.

"Alright, what is it that you have to speak about with my husband?" She almost bit her tongue for being so blunt.

He smiled at her, but his eyes remained serious. Nathanial wasn't aware that this was the very first time Elizabeth had ever met a member of her husband's family.

The handsome stranger didn't answer her question at first but looked her in the eye. When he raised his chin, a slight smile curling his lips, he appeared very similar to her husband.

I'll be darned, the two men really are alike except for their hair and eye color, she mused. *This man is quite a looker but something about him seems to be so grave, yet at the same time wild and untamed.*

The unexpected visitor spoke. "I need John to set the record straight with the family." His voice was very pleasant, but his words confused Elizabeth.

"Set the record straight? What do you mean?"

"I'm so sorry, I haven't even introduced myself. My name is Nathanial Carson, but all my friends and family members call me Nate. I'm John's younger brother."

Elisabeth stared at him suspiciously and almost dropped her glass. "His brother? He has never mentioned a brother." She moved to the far end of the bench, trying to place as much distance as she could between herself and the unknown cowboy.

"I'm not surprised about that. He hasn't behaved very brotherly in the past." Elisabeth remained silent, then she slowly rose.

"Like I told you before, John isn't here today. Come back day after tomorrow if you really want to talk to him." Elizabeth had not expected the stranger to say anything so rude about her husband, and she was quite upset about it.

Nate bit his lower lip and stood up as well. As fast as a flash during a summer storm a thought crossed his mind, and a daring plan took shape in his brain. "You know, thinking about it, I'm afraid that he wouldn't be willing to talk with me, unless there was a powerful reason that would convince him to."

Nate scratched his chin as if he had to think about the situation. Then he bent down and took the basket with the wet laundry that Elizabeth had carried from the river. He walked to the clothesline.

"What in the world are you doing? Put down my laundry immediately." Elizabeth was astonished by the man's behavior, and she glared at him, her cheeks flushed with barely hidden anger.

Nate stood there regarding her, thinking what a beautiful and tempting woman she is. "Ma'am, you have to hang up these clothes or they will start to get moldy."

"Why in Sam Hill would that happen? I will take care of my laundry as soon as you leave our property."

"I'm afraid I can't do that, Mrs. Carson, I will leave, but I won't go alone. You will accompany me."

The words he had spoken hung between them like a dark, threatening cloud. She stared at him in disbelief, her eyes wide and her mouth open.

"The hell I will." She stood in front of him trying hard to appear brave, and for a split second, Nate couldn't help but admire her grit.

Nate turned and hung the wet clothes over the line. He ignored her protest behind his back. Heat rushed through his body when he touched her soft, wet nightgown with his rough hands. She blushed deeply with embarrassment that her personal garment was exposed to the rogue.

"This material is so delicate. The fresh smell of soap is tickling my nose," he mused aloud while touching the material almost tenderly.

What an impossible and rude man. This could never be John's brother, she thought. *John would have told me about him, wouldn't he? What in the world did he mean when he said that he won't leave our ranch alone?* Elizabeth felt deeply worried now.

When the basket was empty, he turned around and looked at her with a stern expression that darkened his handsome features. "Pack a warm jacket and enough provisions for two days. We'll take a ride together."

"You are out of your mind, sir. I will not ride anywhere with you. I order you to leave our property immediately!"

"Well, Ma'am, let me get this straight. I need your help to make sure that John talks to me. I will not harm you, but it is necessary that you cooperate with me now."

As soon as he finished his sentence, he pulled his six-shooter. Shocked, she stared from the weapon in his hand, then into his green eyes. He looked straight into hers, but his features were unreadable, and she had no clue what he would do next. She was certain he meant what he said. *Good Heavens, what am I gonna do now?*

"You can't be serious," she whispered, wringing her hands.

He pointed toward the house with the barrel of his gun. "As I said before, pick up a warm jacket and some food. We will saddle one of your horses and hide out at a place not far from here. I'm pretty sure that John will follow our tracks. You will be safe and reunited with him as soon as he has spoken with me and helped me return to my family. I have no intention of harming you."

"You are nothing but a dang outlaw! My father will

skin you alive when he lays his hands on you." Nathanial laughed at her threat. He had to admit that this lady surprised him. Considering the situation that she was in it, was brave to talk back to him.

Nathanial nudged her toward the house where she reluctantly packed some food and took her warm wool jacket out of the closet. Only the paleness of her face showed how much she feared this man.

Nate wrote a short note on a piece of paper he tore out of the family Bible he found on the shelf behind the table. Elizabeth couldn't believe how ruthless this man was.

He placed the note in the middle of the table and pulled a knife out of its scabbard. She stepped out of the bedroom, and her eyes bulged as she gaped at the knife in his hand. She didn't dare read the note. Tiny beads of sweat showed on her forehead, and her gaze darted nervously between his hand and his face as he stuck the blade right through the middle of the piece of paper, lancing it to the table.

I might have a chance to run him over and throw him off the porch, she thought. But then she realized that he was still aiming his Colt at her and that her husband's rifle hung on a hook on the other side of the room. She quickly gave up on the idea. She walked toward the door, her shoulders sagging, and he followed her.

CHAPTER FIVE

***

HOSTAGE

Nathanial looked down the barrel at Elizabeth, realizing she didn't understand any of this or why he took her as a hostage. But surely, she knew by now he wasn't joking. She obviously didn't know anything about the Carson family secrets, which may give him an advantage.

He commanded her to walk ahead of him toward the corral where the horses were. "Show me which horse is yours so I can saddle it for you. Don't try any tricks. I can assure you that I'm very quick with this here smoke pole, and I won't hesitate to use it, if you make it necessary."

She shook her head, frowning. "I cannot believe you're behaving like this after I was so friendly to you."

"Lady, this is not about you. I have nothing against you, and if my brother sticks to the rules, you will not be harmed. It's a personal thing between John and me. I didn't come here to hurt you. Whether you believe it or not, I generally treat women with respect, ma'am."

She snorted scornfully. "Yes, of course, I can see that

respect very clearly."

His eyes grew wide, as if he couldn't believe what he heard. *She is actually making fun of me. What a daredevil,* he thought. Then an amused smile spread across his face. If circumstances were different, he might try to court her because she was exactly his kind of woman. But that was out of question since she was his brother's wife, and John, unfortunately, was his worst enemy.

When he mounted, he pointed the horse north. He hoped that she could ride well enough so they would get to the place before dark where he had camped the night before.

"Try not to worry too much," he said. "I'm pretty sure you won't be gone from your beautiful home too long." But she didn't look convinced at all. As a matter of fact, she looked quite thoughtful and remained silent.

They had been riding for a couple of hours when Elizabeth started to feel tired. But Nate knew exactly where he was going. As the sun sank behind the woods to their left, they arrived at a small cave that lay hidden in the center of a huge cliff.

She spoke to him for the first time since their ride started. "I reckon you know this place. You must've been hiding here while you planned to kidnap me and threaten John."

Nathanial didn't respond, but thought her voice sounded panicked. *She's giving an awful lot away.*

They dismounted and he pointed toward the cave entrance while he took care of the horses. Elizabeth stood near the opening, looking around. As if he could read her thoughts, he spun around and looked her straight in the eye.

"Don't even think about it. You would never find the way back to your ranch, and there are lots of bears and mountain lions in this area. Besides, it's gonna be dark in about half an hour, and I guess you'll be safer here in this cave."

Although Elizabeth was sometimes more stubborn than a miner's donkey, she nodded slowly, as if admitting to herself that the man was right. He also nodded, satisfied she realized the risks associated with running away would be unnecessary and the outcome unpromising.

Nate watched her. *She seems to be a smart woman, alright.*

With a sigh, she threw up her hands and walked into the cave. Elizabeth's mouth fell open in surprise when she saw the firepit he had prepared inside the cave. He lay warm blankets next to it and built a comfortable-looking pallet where she could sleep. When he saw her puzzled face, he chuckled.

"Did you really think I would tie you to a tree and let you sleep sitting on the ground?" She blushed. He seemed to be able to read her thoughts easily.

"How did you know that I would come with you? Back at our ranch you pretended to kidnap me on the spur of the moment just like the mean, good-for-nothing man that you are."

He didn't seem to have heard her insult. "To be honest, I prepared this firepit for myself two nights ago, and yes, the idea to force you to return here with me was spontaneous. How did I know that you'd obey my order? Well, I aimed my loaded gun at you. That's a mighty strong argument, don't you think? I was pretty certain the daughter of a colonel would be smart enough not to risk her life but would follow my instructions."

Now he had let her know he had obtained information about her family. Anger sparkled in her eyes, and Nate felt quite uncomfortable as she looked particularly pretty at that moment. Embarrassed, he cleared his throat and turned away from her to tend to the campfire.

He took a few supplies from the saddlebags and handed them to her while he got up to fill the coffeepot in the little creek next to the cave. The gurgling water cascaded down from one side of the steep rock cliff.

Nate kneeled at the edge of the clear water and washed his dusty face. He combed back his thick, wavy hair with his wet hands. Single droplets caught the last rays of the setting sun. Elizabeth watched him as he washed, but when he rose and walked toward the campfire, she quickly turned away from him.

After they ate, she held a cup filled with steaming coffee. She already felt the chill of the night, but the steaming beverage warmed her from inside.

She turned to her captor to pump him for information. "So, what is this all about? What happened between you and John?"

She had fired the question at him unexpectedly, and it caught him off guard. He gave her the side eye. "You get straight to the point, don't you?"

She shrugged her shoulders. "What do you expect? You ride out to our place, walk onto our porch, and tell me you are John's brother. John has never mentioned a brother. Of course, I'm surprised. Then you drag me along as your hostage to make sure my husband chases us out here into the wilderness. It seems like you're making all this trouble so you can get him to set some unknown record straight with your family. I do believe I have the right to know what's going on, wouldn't you think so?"

Nate shook his head, wearing an amused smile. "Is there anything at all that might scare you, lady?"

She took a deep breath as she considered his question. "Yes, I fear the day when I lose my father."

Nate regarded her with a thoughtful, although sad expression, his lids half-shut. "I lost mine a few years back. The most devastating fact is that he hasn't died yet but nevertheless, he's unreachable to me."

His words left a puzzled frown on Elizabeth's face. Nate cleared his throat and spilled the beans about what his words meant.

"Many years ago, we all lived happily together on my father's farm. We were a loving family and we all cared about each other until that fateful day when John got into real trouble in town. To be honest, it might be very hurtful for you to learn the truth about him, ma'am."

Elizabeth pulled her shoulders back, looked him straight in the eye, and tried to appear as confident and fearless as possible. The way she held herself showed Nathanial that she had prepared herself for the worst.

How beautiful and brave she looks. Damn it, John, my brother, you have everything in life, don't you? Everything, while I'm condemned to walk through this world alone paying for the sins you committed.

He clenched his teeth as he fought the sudden urge to kiss her. He shook his head in frustration and quickly filled his coffee mug to distract himself. *Jesus, I must be out of my mind.*

Elizabeth sat perfectly still and waited for him to continue with his story. She didn't seem to be scared of him any longer. There was a sadness in his eyes, and her instincts told her that a tragedy had occurred in Nate's family.

For the first time a tiny spark of distrust for her husband showed in her eyes and the frown on her face. "I do recall times when John avoided talking about his family, and I often wondered what he's been hiding," she said quietly. Her gut feeling hardly ever failed her, and now her intuition told her that something in John's life had gone terribly wrong.

Nate imagined that she wouldn't like the story she was about to hear. When he continued his tale, a sadness crept into his voice.

"John had always been father's favorite son, and I had to work extra hard to convince him that I was worthy, too. My mother was generally on my side, but she's not the kind of woman that speaks against her husband.

"John had always been the kind of man who is used to getting what he wants, and he never respected what belonged to another man. If he set his heart on something, he took it. He never wasted a second thought if it already belonged to someone else. It was like that in the past, and I doubt he's changed much since then. He can be quite ruthless, you know."

Elizabeth shook her head in dismay. He was aware that she didn't like what she heard, but Nate continued his story without allowing her to interrupt.

"One late afternoon John went to town. It was cold that day, and he borrowed my new jacket with the warm fur lining. I bought that fine piece only a few days earlier at the local mercantile. As I'm sure you've realized, we're about the same size. None of us knew what he was up to. Later that evening we found out John got himself into a terrible fight. He'd been drinking heavily and began to flirt with the deputy's fiancée. It was a known fact that he had been sweet on the poor girl for weeks. The scene escalated that fateful evening. This time he had crossed the line, and the deputy waited for my brother in the dark alley behind the saloon."

Nate saw Elizabeth shudder on the other side of the fire. "When my brother left the establishment, the law dog confronted him. The deputy intended to teach my brother a lesson with his fists. John always had a violent temper, and this time he completely lost control. The piano music and the crowd were too loud inside the saloon, so none of the guests heard what was going on behind the building, neither did they hear the shot. Couple of months before that fight John bought himself a new Colt and bragged about his sure-shot abilities. It seemed as if he provoked fights on purpose just to try out his new weapon. However, that evening he didn't defend himself in a fair fight. The law dog wasn't armed, and John shot him in cold blood, ruthlessly. Then the coward ran to his horse, gave the stallion the spurs, and came back home. He left the poor man lying in the dirt, bleeding to death behind the town's bodega. But he didn't get away as easily as he thought he would because two men from town witnessed the crime."

Elizabeth stared at him, her eyes wide and her mouth open. "Are you telling me that my husband killed this person on purpose? I don't believe a single word of this." She jumped to her feet and stood next to the fire shaking with fury.

Nate shrugged his shoulders. "Listen, lady, you may not like what I'm telling you, but it's the dang truth. He came riding back to the ranch in a hurry that evening. One of the two witnesses was the owner of the mercantile, and despite John wearing his hat shadowing his face, the trader immediately recognized the jacket John wore. He had sold it to me only a couple of days before. Before we had the slightest idea what was going on, a posse arrived at our property and searched for the villain who shot the deputy. And guess what happened next. They didn't look for John. No, my dear, they searched for me because my brother wore my jacket. To make things worse, the runaway rode my father's palomino stallion which I was known for riding most of the time."

Nathanial's emotions overwhelmed him, and he tried to calm down before continuing the tale. He hadn't spoken about that night in a long time, and it was difficult for him. Bitter emotions he had suppressed for years came back to the surface and stabbed him with many knives.

"I tried to defend myself and begged my father and the members of the posse to believe that I hadn't been in town at all that day or evening. I tried everything to convince them that I wasn't the kind of curly wolf that would shoot an unarmed man. But my father turned away from me. He looked as if he was disgusted by the sight of me, and he declared before everyone that I was no longer his son."

Elizabeth listened in fascination to the tale of her husband's family, even though it told of reprehensible acts she didn't think the man she married was capable of committing.

Nate's voice shook. "Can you imagine? My father didn't give me the slightest chance to prove my innocence or to explain where I had been before the incident behind the saloon took place. I'll never forget the way he looked at me, revulsion twisting his features."

Nathanial's voice was barely more than a whisper by then and tears pooled in his eyes. He was hardly able to hold them back.

Elizabeth didn't know what to say. She was truly shocked at the things he told her. He could see it was hard for her to believe this story. Emotional turmoil reflected on her beautiful face.

"But I'm sure that John told the truth to the posse, didn't he? After all, shooting the deputy could have been judged as some sort of self-defense because the other fellow waited to attack John behind the saloon. Talk, for Christ's sake. Tell me the truth!"

Nate raised his gaze from the flames of the campfire and looked at her, his face serious. Elizabeth recognized the truth before he uttered another word. His eyes told her the answer. As he slowly shook his head, his features showed the disappointment and anger he felt about the unexpected betrayal years ago. He had been carrying that pain buried like a thorn in his heart for nine long years.

"No, he just stood there while I waited, hoping desperately that this boot-licker of a brother would tell them the truth. But he remained silent. It would have been easy for him to save me, but he double-crossed me. He took the jacket off before coming into the house, so no one but me had seen him wearing it. John let me down as if I was a stranger—me, his own brother. He pretended to be as innocent as an old maid in Sunday church."

Nate looked at the ground and kicked the dirt with his boots. "He must have been aware that the townsfolk wouldn't hesitate to hang me from the next tree. They were a furious mob, and they wouldn't wait for a trial. The murdered law dog was well liked among the men in town, and his friends were out for revenge."

Elizabeth remained silent, her face pale. Her deep hurt at these unbelievable accusations had the corners of her mouth turned down and her eyebrows drooping with sadness. "Is this all a big bluff, or are you making a real play? I can't believe that John would commit such a terrible crime and run away like a coward. Why would he deliver his own brother to the hangman? John is a man of honor."

Nate snorted at the word "honor." "This tale might not fit into your image of the man you married. But, believe me, he is nothing but a shack, a scoundrel."

She remembered John remaining silent when the topic of his family came up. And there were the countless times when he had cleaned his beloved Colt and seemed totally lost in thought. Handling that gun put up a wall around him, and he reacted to nothing and nobody, not even her.

She had gotten used to it, but now she saw those facts in a different light, and they started to make sense. Several times she had tried to convince him to visit his parents. When she did, he always reacted impatiently, even aggressively, toward her. Last time she tried to talk him into it, he started a nasty argument, yelling at her for the first time in their relationship.

The beautiful woman sat beside the campfire, lost in thought. "I know nearly nothing about the man I married," she whispered. "I trusted him blindly from the very first day."

Nate studied her pale face and sad eyes. Her lost look triggered pity in him. He battled the sudden urge to give her a hug, expecting that she would push him away. "Don't blame yourself. He's always been a spark who could sweet talk himself into people's lives."

Nathanial knew that he had hurt her deeply by showing up at her home and revealing an unbearable truth about her husband. *Seems like that coward has hidden the truth from her just like he never spoke truthfully to my parents or admitted the crime to men of the law.* Nate wasn't surprised at all. John had always been a selfish man.

"What happened next?" Elizabeth asked, her voice shaking. Slowly she moved closer to the campfire and sat on a flat rock, holding out her hands to warm them.

Nate wondered if she would ever be able to look at her man the same loving way or would she always see a stranger who had murdered a man and gotten away with it? *She must be really worried about the future of her marriage now,* he mused.

Nate continued his story. "When I realized that I would end up in prison or most likely with a rope around my neck, I tried to escape. I knew that the palomino stood behind the house still saddled. I jumped through the window and landed on the porch. From there I vaulted straight into the saddle and gave that horse the spurs as if the devil himself was after me. I guess nobody expected me to run, but I had only one chance to escape. Nobody believed my side of the story. I must have taken them by surprise because it took a couple of minutes before they jumped into their saddles to chase me."

The fire in the cave burned low and Elizabeth threw another log on it. She listened intently to Nate's story about his family.

"You know, from childhood on I had a special passion for exploring caves, and I knew all of them in our area. Just a few days prior to that fateful evening I found a small cave near my father's corn fields. I would never have thought that my passion for underground tunnels would save my life one day. I hid myself and my horse in that dark hole. Since it was late evening, the men from the posse couldn't see my tracks. Later that night the rain erased them for good."

Now it was Nate's turn to warm his hands and he stretched them toward the flames. "I will never forget how cold I was, but building a fire was too great a risk. I still dream of the nerve-wracking sound of water dripping through the cave's ceiling. I still feel the shame of hiding alongside the fear of getting caught. Almost every night the pain caused by my father and my brother tortures me. I know I can't return to my parents unless the truth is told at last. Good grief, I haven't seen them in nine years. Nine lonely years. Then, the night after my escape, I sneaked out of the cave and left my home soil for good. I rode west and made a living working as wrangler for a while. I joined the army for a few years."

Elizabeth's face reflected her emotions. Her eyes were bloodshot, and tears ran down her cheeks. Her old world as she knew it after marrying John shattered into pieces like a glass pitcher dropped to the ground. Sudden anger took control of her, and she yelled at Nathanial "Why now? Why are you looking for your brother now? Why are you threatening us?"

A smile played on his lips as he regarded her before answering. "As I told you before, I haven't seen my family in nine years. I miss my parents. My life has been terribly lonely the past few years. Rumor has it that my father is sick with consumption. I'm sure my mother suffers tremendously with the situation as she has to take care of him and the farm since both of her sons have left home. It's impossible for her to handle it all alone. My father is most likely going to die pretty soon. That's a sad fact. All I wish is that they finally discover the truth and that we can forgive each other before Dad has to leave this world. As far as I know, John left the farm shortly after my escape and never told them the truth about what really happened. At least, that's what I heard. That's the reason I'm forced to rely on such radical methods to convince him to talk to our parents. Holding you hostage is the only way to make him come along back to my parents. At least I hope he will."

Elizabeth shook her head. She was devastated and felt bone tired. She got up and went over to the spot he had prepared for her so she could sleep warm close to the fire. The chances of running away and returning safely to their ranch were zero, especially since he had hobbled the horses close to where he sat.

Elizabeth curled up under the blanket and closed her

eyes. She didn't want to talk any longer. Nathanial was sure that she couldn't stand hearing more of this depressing story. He understood very well how she felt. He wasn't at all offended that she wanted to avoid further conversation, but he felt sympathy for her.

It must be devastating to find out that her beloved husband was nothing but a ruthless killer and a coward, he mused.

Nate knew his brother quite differently from the way Elizabeth knew him. *Will I ever be able to forgive him?*

He shrugged off his thoughts and walked over to the entrance to pick up his saddle. He carried it closer to the fire to use it as his headrest.

The extra blanket tied to the pommel caught his attention. *I don't need more than one. She might get cold in the night.* He unfolded it and covered her with it. She looked up at him with her sad eyes and thanked him softly. Then she turned over.

Nathanial sat down next to his saddle and stared into the flames. *Will he come searching for his wife? God knows, I'm scared to meet my brother again. What if he loses his temper just like that time back home?* It might be worse now since it's about his own wife.

Trapped between the thoughts that kept him awake and the nightmares that pursued him when he dozed off, Nathanial passed a restless night.

CHAPTER SIX

***

WAITING TO BE RESCUED!

The following day Elizabeth woke early. She struggled to open her eyes and get out of bed. *How long will John take to rescue me? I just want to get home as quickly as possible to my own little world. But will it still be the same happy life that we've built?*

Elizabeth knew she would demand answers from her spouse. If they were to continue living together, she had to know the truth. How she would deal with that truth she didn't yet know.

Nate was already up and poking through the remaining embers to get the fire going again. He pointed to a small path that led away from the cave. "I'm sure you want to relieve yourself. There are some rocks farther down the path that will grant you some privacy."

Her cheeks turned hot and red. She quickly pulled up her skirt and followed the tiny trail. When she returned, he handed her a clean piece of cloth and a chunk of nice smelling soap.

"I'll lead the horses to a meadow close by to let them graze and water them farther down the creek. You'll have the camp all to yourself for at least half an hour. That should give you enough time to wash yourself without being disturbed. After that we can eat some breakfast. I'm not functioning well without my dose of morning cowboy coffee," he added with a boyish smile. Despite feeling very insecure around him she couldn't help but smile back.

She watched him as he walked away from the camp toward a field swaying with tall grass. The two horses followed him immediately. His figure was slim but with well-defined muscles. His long, wavy hair brushed over his shoulder as he turned his head to the horse to his left and patted its neck tenderly.

Puzzled, she looked down at the soap in her hand. She couldn't see through this man. "I have every reason in this world to be upset and angry with this guy. Most likely, I should fear him. He threatened me with a loaded gun and dragged me into this wilderness against my will. But despite all that, he's thoughtful enough to cover me with his own blanket so I won't feel cold and to leave me alone so I can have a bath in private. For Heaven's sake, how did I get myself into this mess?" she mumbled.

She walked over to the creek and put the soap and the cloth on a rock next to it. After braiding her hair, she waded carefully into the cool water and dipped the cloth in the stream. The soap in her hand had a fresh smell like wildflowers. She scrubbed herself clean.

When he returned with the animals, she already had the pot of coffee boiling on the embers. He was relieved to see that she had not tried to run away. He watched her setting the two cups on the flat rock next to the firepit, pouring some of the strong brew into each one of them. He added some sugar to his coffee, and the rich taste tickled his senses. "Just like I prefer my coffee, strong enough to float your Colt in it."

Elizabeth noticed Nate staring at a wet strand of hair sticking to her neck, and he swallowed hard. *He shouldn't be staring at me, his brother's wife, like that.* She frowned at him. He swallowed again and looked away rapidly, knowing he had been caught admiring her womanly charms.

Elizabeth wondered if his attraction to her might derail his plan of forcing his brother to return home with him. She wondered if she could use it to her advantage.

Nathanial walked over to the sack with supplies and came back with some bread and beef jerky. He handed some to her, including the small cotton bag holding sugar for her coffee. He nodded when she refilled his cup with the hot, steaming beverage and for a brief moment their fingertips touched.

She held his gaze, and he stared at her sensually shaped lips. But then he quickly turned away and peered into the flames of the campfire. Elizabeth could see she was tempting him. *I hope my plan doesn't backfire, and he goes too far.*

He sat on the stone next to the firepit and passed some of the jerky to her. They both ate in silence, caught up in their own thoughts about the uncomfortable situation.

"When do you expect John to be back at the ranch?" His sudden question almost made her jump.

She shrugged her shoulders. "He wanted to return this afternoon, at latest tomorrow around noontime. It's always difficult to plan ahead as one never knows how long you need for a cattle roundup, but I'm sure you know much better than me about handling cattle."

A boyish grin appeared on his handsome features. He liked her dark humor although he had to admit that sometimes he felt like tanning her hide for talking back sarcastically. The thought of it amused him, but he wondered if it wouldn't be better for him to cool down in the creek next to the cave.

***

Back at Elizabeth's home a small dust cloud settled behind the gate of the Carson ranch. John dismounted and wrapped the reins around the porch pole. He walked toward the main door and called for Elizabeth.

They were able to finish work almost a full day earlier than expected, and John had hurried to get back home. He wanted to continue working with the new stallion. The magnificent animal would be an enormous asset for his herd. The stallion's physique was impressive, packed with muscles. His shiny black coat gleamed in the sunshine.

"Elizabeth, darling, I'm home." There was no answer. Puzzled he turned around and scratched his chin. *"Maybe she went to town to visit her father,"* he mused.

John walked to the water pump and held his head under the stream of cold water. He brushed back his wet, brown hair and decided to go for a glass of cold lemonade before getting started at the corral. He noticed that Elizabeth's horse was not there. So, he must have guessed right that she was in town.

When he stepped into the house and turned toward the kitchen, he saw a piece of paper on the table. His heart skipped a beat. He didn't read the note at first, once he saw the knife that held it pinned to the wooden table. He recognized it immediately. His heart pounded at a rapid rate, hammering inside his ribcage. *Was this possible*?

John touched the handle of the knife gingerly. It was formed from deer antler and sported the familiar carving on one side. Instinctively, John touched his own knife hanging in the beautiful leather scabbard Elizabeth had given him for his last birthday. John knew the carving by heart. His initials and a small deer head had been artfully chiseled on the handle. Both knives were identical except for the initials and had been gifts from a father to his two sons. Nathanial owned the same knife as John did.

Finally, he read the note.

> *"You have always been the superior tracker of us two. If you want to see your wife again you better make sure that you find us without a posse at your tail. You know exactly what I want from you. You have to set the record straight. You owe it to me. I have the same right to be with my family as you do. Nine years on the run is more than enough, don't you think?*
>
> Nate.*"*

John stood bewildered, holding the piece of paper as sweat rolled down his forehead. "Oh Lord, he's got Elizabeth," he whispered. John didn't know what Nate would do with her, or even worse, what he would tell her.

The rancher cursed and tossed the knife away. It skidded across the wood table, fell over the edge, and landed under John's chair. Nobody heard either his cussing, or the eerie silence that followed.

Should I inform Elizabeth's father? He could help me set up a posse in no time. But he shook his head. *I'm sure my brother has developed into one tough man. Otherwise, he would have never gotten this far.*

John fell into his chair with his face in his hands as he

realized that his past had caught up with him. After all those years had passed, he had not expected to meet his brother again. Only John and Nate knew the truth about the events of that ill-fated evening nine years ago.

John raised his fist as anger replaced despair. "I will search for Nate and Elizabeth by myself. John Carson doesn't need a posse or help from others to solve his problems," he growled. Furious, he grabbed his favorite Colt and checked the bullets. The blued barrel reflected the afternoon sun as it sent its rays through the kitchen window. Since he owned that fine weapon, he had never failed to hit what he aimed at and he wouldn't this time either.

After refreshing himself under the water pump he changed into a new shirt. He filled his canteen with fresh water and packed a few supplies and a warm blanket. Less than half an hour later he mounted a different horse and galloped toward the mountains.

"This time you won't escape, brother," he swore, shaking his fist and scowling.

After a few minutes, he found the tracks of the two horses leading away from the ranch. One of the animals left the typical prints of an Indian pony as it wasn't shoed. He was quite certain that it was Elizabeth's mare which had been given to them as a wedding gift by the Indians living next to the fort. The tracks led him to the mountain range north of his property. John pushed his horse to a fast gallop and prepared mentally for the worst…

***

For the captive, the afternoon crawled by. Nate had collected more firewood and shot a rabbit for dinner. Elizabeth tried her best to prepare a decent meal from it. There was nothing else that she could do except wait for her husband. Despite Nathanial's friendliness, she was still a hostage in this cave.

Nathanial didn't have anything to do with his time except admire his captive. Her red hair reflected the late afternoon sun, and her sparkling eyes reminded him of the blue sky in the open prairie. It was easy to see that she had Irish blood in her, and her delicate features stood in sharp contrast with her daring, almost stubborn behavior. *She has the temperament of a prospector's stick of dynamite with a short fuse to light it.*

Sudden jealousy hit Nathanial like a punch in the gut. He envied his brother for marrying this wonderful woman. His entire life John seemed to get the biggest piece of cake. That particular moment Nate hated him from the bottom of his heart. He added some firewood to the flames as he tried to bring his emotions under control.

This sudden desire for Elizabeth confused Nate. He had learned to hide his feelings. Otherwise, he would have never made it through the nine years of loneliness and despair in his life as a homeless saddle tramp. Usually, it wasn't difficult for him to suppress his emotions or the desire to see his family again. But Elizabeth seemed to march right through his wall of emotional self-protection.

Elizabeth took a few potatoes out of her saddlebag and tossed them into the embers, then she skinned the rabbit. She put the animal into a big iron pan and let it fry in its own fat along with some wild onions and herbs she had collected along the creek. It didn't take long, and an appetizing smell drifted through the cave.

Nate walked over to the streambed and took off his shirt. He scooped water over his shoulders and chest muscles. It was cold but refreshing, and for a couple of minutes he forgot about the woman in the cave next to the fire. A satisfied smile curled his lips when his horse walked toward him and started to lick the water drops from his deeply tanned shoulders. His loud laughter echoed from the cliff, and he scratched the beautiful stallion under his mane. He adored the animal and took good care of him.

Elizabeth watched the scene and smiled. That particular moment, Nate didn't seem to be a dangerous man at all.

The last rays of the setting sun were caught by countless tiny water drops on his back. They glittered like little diamonds and emphasized the smoothness of his skin.

She stood there staring at his muscular chest and the tiny line of curly soft hair that grew below his belly button and disappeared behind his belt. His stomach was flat and packed with muscles, looking as if it had been chiseled.

He noticed her gawking, and his eyes held hers. An amused, knowing smile appeared on his handsome features. Her cheeks blushed an even darker shade of red, and she quickly turned to face the fire so she could tend the food.

She muttered aloud, "What in the Sam Hill am I thinking, admiring the body of the very person who kidnapped me? Am I completely out of my mind?" She wasn't aware that she was talking to herself.

"Food will be ready in a few minutes," she said more loudly, but her voice was high pitched, strained, and gave away her excitement. Pretending not to notice, he turned and grabbed his shirt from the rock. Slowly, as if to tease her, he pulled it over his wet chest.

Nate hoped that she hadn't realized how much emotional turmoil her gaze caused in him. To feel the look of her eyes on his skin had triggered a desire that he had not felt in a very long time.

He slowly walked back into the cave and noticed a wonderful aroma coming from the firepit. "That smells delicious. How in the world did you manage to prepare such a fine meal under such primitive circumstances out here in the wilderness?"

She smiled. "My mother was a fantastic cook. She taught me a lot before she died."

"Oh, I'm so sorry," he said, staring at his feet. He seemed embarrassed about reminding her of her late mother. He had two sides—the charming and sometimes boyish man and a dangerous, yet attractive feller who battled his own demons.

She recalled the memory of his bare torso, and guilt swept over her like a cold wave. She lowered her gaze, and he knew what she had been thinking about. A loud growling sound from Nate's stomach interrupted the embarrassing silence stretching between the two of them. Both laughed and relaxed.

"Sounds as if somebody's really hungry," Elizabeth said, smiling so that her dimples showed. He nodded and slapped his tummy as he smiled back at her.

They enjoyed their food and told each other tales from their childhood. Nathanial avoided talking about John and Elizabeth didn't ask further about him. Nate was aware that his brother never told her anything about his family, and he was sympathetic toward her. *When two people love each other but can't share everything, how can their marriage be trusting?* he wondered.

When he told her the story how he sneaked into the priest's orchard to steal apples and fell out of a tree, she chuckled. Her laughter sounded like a bell on a peaceful Sunday morning and charmed him. The experience of sitting and talking with her warmed him inside. He found he really enjoyed her company.

Nate got up to fetch some fresh water for their coffee. Elizabeth seemed less afraid and more relaxed. Except for threatening her with a loaded six-shooter, so far, he had treated her with respect.

Most likely she'll insist John tell her the truth this time, Nate thought as he walked back to the fire. In Nate's opinion, the fact that her husband hadn't told her important facts about his past was almost as bad as lying to her face. Lies of omission open the door to distrust between lovers. Nate was the kind of man who believed in being honest all the time, even if it hurts worse than the sting of a wasp.

Elizabeth was the daughter of a colonel who had been brought up with the highest respect for law, order, and honor. He figured she didn't know what scared her more—that her husband might face punishment once the crime he'd committed was discovered or the damage that his lies had done to their relationship.

***

When it grew too dark to read their tracks, John set up camp for the night. He was quite certain that Nate wouldn't harm Elizabeth. After all he wanted him and not his wife. His brother wouldn't be so foolish to throw away the only high card in his hand.

***

A cruel smile formed on the face of the pursuer as he poked the logs of his campfire. He mumbled into the darkness, "Well, little brother, we shall see if I tell our parents the truth, or if you are going to bitterly regret that you set foot onto my property. Daring to holding my wife hostage and interfering in my new life I've built from scratch is going too far. I'll make sure you regret the day you came to our ranch." Then he covered himself with a warm blanket, using his saddle as a headrest, and slept. He didn't touch the supplies in his saddlebag…

***

The fire had burned down to only a few embers gleaming in the cold gloom of the cave. Elizabeth shook as if she were freezing. Her sleep had been interrupted by terrible nightmares of pursuit and captivity. She watched Nate sleeping on the other side of the firepit and wished for her warm ranch house.

The leftover embers didn't warm her, and she rose to retrieve some of the firewood that Nate had piled next to the entrance of their hideout. With a sigh she flipped back the blanket and got up.

When she took a step toward the firewood, she accidentally stepped on a dry branch that snapped with a loud crack under her foot. Nathanial jumped to his feet, aiming his gun at her. She froze, crouching, staring at him. Her eyes went wide, and her mouth flew open. The moon cast her silvery light into the cave, and Nate saw the fear reflected on her beautiful face.

"Where do you think you're going?" he growled at her. *Most likely she wants to take one of the horses and try to escape,* he thought. "Don't be such a fool, you wouldn't make it anyway."

She lowered her chin. A few strands of hair had escaped the thick braid. Her hands clenched into small fists. "I'm asking myself who might be the bigger fool out of the two of us in this God forsaken cave." she yelled. "I wanted to get some firewood because I'm freezing to death. Instead of being at home in my warm comfortable bed I'm out here in this dang wilderness where you barbarian saphead dragged me. And now you're standing here, threatening me again with your loaded gun, although I'm trying to keep your sorry ass warm as well."

He stood before her like a small boy that had just been

scolded by his own mother and was dumbfounded. She stood across from him, her face red with fury and her breathing heavy as if she had just run a mile. She was madder than a cat thrown into water.

A low moan escaped his lips. She had never looked more beautiful and tempting to him than in this very moment.

Nate took a careful step toward her but couldn't believe his eyes when she raised her fist and feinted a punch. The man was flabbergasted. She looked like she could scratch his eyes out. They stared at each other with sparks of anger flying between them like cinders from a fire.

As she shook with fury, the loaded barking iron in his hand suddenly made him nervous. *Good Heavens, what if she really attacks me. My weapon could discharge accidently. She might be crazy enough to do such a thing.*

He clicked the hammer back into secure position but kept it aimed at her a moment longer as Elizabeth glared at him like a rattlesnake ready to strike. Her fist was still in midair, and he wouldn't have been astonished if she landed a painful hook on his chin.

Sudden rage took hold of him. Not because she held her fist in the ready position to punch him but because of the uncontrollable desire she triggered in him. He had successfully suppressed such emotions for a long time, but this redheaded she-devil plowed through his self-control with no difficulty. The built-up walls of self-protection crumbled under her laughter like last Sunday's teatime cake.

Nathanial took a deep breath and tossed the revolver onto his blanket. He reached Elizabeth with two steps of his long, powerful legs. He reached for her wrist and bent it roughly behind her.

She stepped back, alarmed by his brutish approach. Bracing herself on her left foot, she tried to kick his shin with her right, but she was no match for his strength. He bent down and kissed her roughly on her mouth. She struck his chest with her slender hands, but he held her tightly.

After a long moment, the pressure of his mouth lessened. His tongue caressed her lower lip tenderly. Although she had been struggling against his embrace, he felt her trembling as he held her. With a sigh she parted her lips, opening to him. He kissed her more passionately while holding her in his strong arms.

For a few seconds his thoughts protested, trying to get control over the dangerous situation, but it was too late. Desire for this woman crashed over him like a tsunami, and his heart hammered against his ribcage. *Dear God, how sweet her lips taste.*

He was unable to deny his rising passion because his body spoke a clear language. He could fool neither her nor himself. *She must feel it as she presses herself against me.*

It was Elizabeth who managed to pull away from him, but she needed every ounce of her strong willpower to do so. She panted and her eyes stared into his, bewildered and confused. She rubbed her hand over her lips as if she could undo the kiss. But no word escaped her. What could she have said?

Nathanial could see the shock of kissing him written all over her beautiful face. He was her husband's brother who had presented such a danger to her and her marriage. But the racing pulse under the delicate skin besides her throat gave away the truth that the kiss had affected her physically as much as it had Nathanial.

She turned away from him, her eyes full of tears as redness spread through her cheeks. He stood there silently and didn't know what to say.

When he finally spoke, his voice sounded hoarse,

reflecting the arousal he felt. "I am so sorry, Elizabeth. I really don't know what got into me. It wasn't my intention to treat you disrespectfully."

She faced him, her eyes wide and her lower jaw opening and closing. She pointed at his nose, elbow bent, as if she were scolding him. "That will never happen again, you hear me?"

"Yes, ma'am," he answered quietly, yet he knew that he wasn't sure if he could keep that promise.

Elizabeth went over to her sleeping place but turned her back to him. She lay awake, staring into the dark, curved ceiling of the cave reflecting the firelight. Nate sat next to the fire. He made sure that it burned the entire night because he didn't want her to be freezing again.

Sleep? He was too perturbed to consider about it. The lady who slept on the other side of the firepit challenged his feelings more than any other female had before. *Land sake's alive, does it have to be John's wife? Out of all the women in the world, why her? As if the rift between him and me isn't big enough already.*

In the wee hours, Nate fell into a slumber that was haunted by nightmares about his father chasing him out of the house while his brother's cruel laughter followed him.

***

John rolled out of his blanket with the first daylight peeping over the top of the mountains. He saddled his horse and followed the tracks that let directly to a lower mountain ridge. Pine trees grew at the bottom of it.

The man's face was grim, and his eyes held a cold glitter. He reached a small deer path and bent over the saddle to study the clearly visible tracks. They seemed fresh, so he slowed down his horse while carefully examining the trail as he rode along it.

After a while the trees cleared, and a massive red-hued rock cliff appeared around the next bend. John dismounted and shaded his eyes against the glaring morning sun. He saw a dark spot in the middle of the cliff and wondered if it could be an opening in the rock. Suddenly he recalled Nate's fascination for caves. "I bet that you haven't changed some of your old habits, have you, little brother?"

Carefully John picked the best route to get as close to the presumed cave as possible without being seen from above. He was quite sure that his wife was up there. Nevertheless, he didn't hurry. This was about Nathanial and their past. His brother had challenged him, which was bad enough. Beyond that, he was quite certain that Nathanial had told Elizabeth all kinds of foolish stories about what happened before he left the Carson family.

Unfortunately, John's wife was his second priority now. John wouldn't allow anybody to destroy what he built up, not even a member of his own family. After the betrayal, family counted less than anybody to John.

He sneaked through the trees as he had no clue how well his younger brother had developed his fighting skills during the past few years. John knew he had to be careful, and it would be an advantage to get as close as possible to the cave's entrance before Nate noticed him.

John left his horse behind, tying the reigns to a tree. The mare and Nate's horse up by the cave would neigh when they caught the scent of his gelding. John didn't want them warning his brother of his approach.

The hollow was in clear sight now and seemed big enough for hiding two people and their horses. John knew that confronting his brother was unavoidable and wondered if he could shoot at his own flesh and blood. When he thought about it again, he had to admit that that Nate hasn't meant anything to him for years. There were no brotherly feelings as there were between most siblings. He knew he could draw against Nate.

***

Nate had already washed himself at the creek before Elizabeth awoke. He'd watered the horses, and the aroma of freshly brewed coffee wafted throughout their hideout.

"Good morning," she mumbled shyly. He nodded back at her, a friendly smile lingering on his face. An uncomfortable silence hung between the two. As they ate their bacon and beans and sipped their hot coffee, no conversation developed.

Nate cleared his throat. "Listen, about yesterday—"

She raised her hand, interrupting him, and he went silent. When she spoke, she looked him directly in the eye.

"I kissed you back. So, if there is any reason to apologize then I would have to do the same, wouldn't I?"

At first, he didn't answer but took a sip from his coffee and washed down the last bite of his bacon. *I'm not hungry anyway.* But that was a blunt lie. He was hungry but it wasn't for food. The redhead sitting opposite him had triggered off a desire. He had been thinking about her most of the night. Yes, he desired that woman and if circumstances weren't so complicated, he would have tried whatever he could to conquer her heart.

Nate had cursed his destiny countless times during the past few hours. He was certain that John didn't deserve such an exceptional woman, but who was he to judge him? Nate was nothing but a homeless saddle tramp who had fallen from grace. So, all he could do was keep his admiration a secret, and pretend the kiss was based on nothing but raw attraction.

If his plan worked out, they would separate in a few days, and he would most likely never see her again. Although he knew that it would be for the best for both of them, the thought of never meeting her again bothered him.

Nate wasn't a fool. He knew that he couldn't conquer her heart. She would always see him as a threat to her husband and her marriage. Besides, Nathanial had never felt good in the role of an intruder into someone else's relationship. It was against his basic rules and not his kind of game.

He caught sight of how sad his face looked in the mirror he used to trim his beard. He got up walked over to the entrance to gaze at the landscape below them, lost in thought.

CHAPTER SEVEN

* * *

CAIN AND ABEL

A shout made them jump. They recognized the voice immediately, so well-known to them both. "Nate. Are you up there? Show yourself, you coward."

Elizabeth jumped to her feet. "John! It's John." Nate quickly pulled his revolver, and she stopped dead in her tracks. He wouldn't let her run through the cave entrance. "You stay right where you are, Elizabeth."

She wanted to rush to her husband but obeyed the commanding presence of the loaded gun. She seemed uncertain, not knowing if he would really shoot her.

Nate raised his hand and motioned that she should remain silent. He whispered, "Elizabeth, please. We don't know if he'll start shooting right away as soon as one of us walks through that entrance into daylight. I don't want you to get hurt."

She stared at him in amazement, but she knew he was right. It was a dangerous situation, but would John really shoot at his own brother? Unfortunately, neither she nor

Nate knew what John was capable of. After all, Nate had kidnapped his wife. Chances were good that he would react unpredictably, like an injured mountain lion.

She didn't move, wringing her hands while she waited. A furious John Carson yelled again. "Nate, are you in this God forsaken cave? Answer, you scum."

John's voice oozed with contempt and fury. His loud voice echoed from the cliff again.

"Nate, answer me immediately. Elisabeth, darling, are you up there?" She begged her kidnapper, her eyes huge, to be allowed to answer her husband. He nodded. "I'm here John. I'm okay. He didn't harm me."

"Let her go, Nate." John yelled toward the opening in the rock wall, not answering his wife. Nate moved very carefully. He was smart enough not to walk straight into the line of fire. Nathanial didn't trust his brother, and who could blame him for it? John had let him down when he needed him most, if the story Nate told Elizabeth was true.

Nate turned around and whispered, "Whatever happens now you have to stay away from the cave mouth." She nodded and he carefully peeked outside.

Nate's voice was quieter. "Show yourself. Take off your holster with the gun in it. Hold your rig way above your head so I can see it." The sound of heavy boots crunching on loose gravel alarmed both the people inside the cave. John was much closer to the entrance than they assumed.

"What do you want from me, Nate?"

The younger brother shook his head, dismay clouding his features. "You know exactly what I want, John, I want you to ride to our parents with me and tell them the truth. It's about time that they got to know who really shot the deputy nine years ago."

"And why do you think I would do that? Give me

one reason why I should risk getting arrested and end up dangling from a leafless tree for you?"

"For me? You must be kidding. If you get arrested, it's for your own crime. I haven't done anything wrong, John. You know that. The only crime I committed was to hold your wife hostage to make sure you would follow us. I swear to God, I haven't harmed her. You know the truth. You know that you shot that poor unarmed feller."

Elizabeth was convinced that the two brothers would be able to talk things over and finally settle the fight that had been standing between them for so many years. She believed her father's philosophy that folks can talk their way through to a peaceful solution.

"All right, Nate. I'll take my gun belt off and come into the cave. Let's talk."

Elizabeth was relieved. Everything would be alright soon. Nathanial stood next to the fire and waited for his brother, whom he hadn't seen for nine years. John carried his gun holster in his left hand. Nate aimed his revolver at him and pointed over to the flat rock close to the fire. John Carson looked over at his wife. "Are you okay?"

She smiled at him. "Yes, dear, I'm alright. I sure am happy to see you." John turned and stared at Nate. His eyes had adjusted to the semidarkness in the cavern, and he studied the face of his younger brother.

Nathanial had changed. The once innocent-looking boy had developed into a handsome man with broad shoulders. His hair was much longer than it used to be, and he sported a well-trimmed beard that gave him a more mature look. They held each other's gaze without blinking. *Wonder what he thinks of me after all the hard work I've done,* Nate thought. *I'm not a scrawny kid anymore.*

Despite the older one's wrongdoing, Nate was happy

to see him. *There must be some truth in it when folks say that blood is thicker than water.*

John, on the other hand, viewed his brother with eyes cold as ice and showed no emotions at all, his face unreadable. Nate wondered if Elizabeth had seen her loving husband like this before, and what she thought of him at this moment.

Nate broke the prolonged silence hanging between the three of them. "John, Father is sick. The coughing sickness will get the best of him soon. I want you to accompany me and explain to him what happened that fateful night." Nate didn't beat around the bush. John walked over to the fire and sat down on a rock close by.

"That dog won't hunt, Nate. You're holding my wife hostage. And now you want me to put my neck into a hangman's noose. That is the biggest piece of balderdash you ever came up with."

"Pull in your horns, brother. You owe it to me. You know that I never would've harmed your wife. But I want to return to my family. Unlike you, I really miss my parents, and I want to make sure that father is at peace when he meets our Lord and Savior."

John's cold, cruel laughter gave Elizabeth the chills. She was shocked at her husband's reaction, and for the first time he seemed like a stranger to her. The two men acted as if they had forgotten that Elizabeth stood close by. She felt as if she were invisible on the other side of the firepit.

John bent down, picked up a stick and poked the embers that glowed below the ashes. When he spoke, his voice carried a harsh, controlled undertone that made him sound dangerous.

"Nate, I will not go anywhere with you, and I will not set any record straight. You had your chance to escape and start a new life. You should have remained in hiding. It would have been best for all of us. But you had to catch the wrong wolf by the ears, didn't you? If you came to my ranch seeking justice, I will be disappointing you. There is no so-called justice, little brother. Out there the law of the wolfpack rules this world."

He pointed out of the cave to emphasize his words. "Only the strongest survive. Believe me, Nathanial, I have always been and will always be the stronger one. You're meant to be the loser."

Nate stared daggers at his brother, his hate boiling over. "You're nothing but a dang coward. You didn't have the sand to stand by your own crime nine years ago, and you don't have the backbone now to admit that you shot that unarmed law dog. But I know the truth, and you're nailed to the counter for your lies."

John shrugged his shoulders, not giving a damn about his brother's confrontations. "By hook or by crook, in any case I'll be the one who survives, not you."

The words hung between the two brothers like the dark cloud of a thunderstorm. Then several things happened in the blink of an eye. While still poking the ashes with the stick in his right hand, John used his left to pull his blued Colt out of the holster where it lay on the flat rock by the fire.

He had always been proud that his aim was equally excellent with both hands. He drew and aimed the six-shooter at his brother in one swift, fluid motion and pulled the trigger. The shot rang through the cave, its deadly echo rebounded multiple times by the rock walls.

Elizabeth screamed, her hands covering her pale face. Nathanial's features showed first his disbelief followed by a mask of pure pain. A loud groan escaped his gaping mouth as his eyes squeezed closed. He pressed his left hand to his ribcage, blood leaking between his fingers as a red stain spread rapidly on his shirt. His knees buckled, and he fell to the ground.

Elizabeth took a few steps toward where Nate lay, but she stopped, regarding her husband. "For Heaven's sake, what have you done, John? You shot your own brother." She looked at Nate on the ground, his face waxen, not moving. Was he dead? Elizabeth was covered her mouth and held her waist, feeling sick to her stomach. The horror of what she had just witnessed lay heavily on her.

John walked toward her, the smoking gun still in his hand. Elizabeth rushed toward him. She wanted him to hold her tight and wake her from this nightmare. But there was something in his eyes that held her back. Instead of embracing her he stared at her with a frown on his face.

"John, what's the matter? We must inform the Marshal. Nothing will happen to you. We will claim it was self-defense. After all, he held me hostage, right?"

John shook his head. "Maybe that would work with that tin star feller. But there is a hair in the butter, dear. Even if I get away with self-defense, it wouldn't change the fact that you know the truth. And to make it even worse, now you know my past as well."

He seemed to be pondering that thought. Elizabeth watched him, puzzled, and it took a few seconds before she realized what his words meant. "He told the truth, didn't he?" Her voice was barely more than a whisper. "You really shot that deputy nine years ago and put the blame on your brother, didn't you? You would have never told me the truth if he hadn't showed up, right?"

As he watched her, for a brief moment a look of sorrow scurried across his face. But that sympathy disappeared as fast as a flame is extinguished in the wind.

"I'm really sorry, Elizabeth, but I can't allow anyone to know the truth about me. It would ruin everything that I've built. Your oh-so-proud father with his ridiculous high moral standards about law and honor would have me hung by a military tribunal in the blink of an eye. No, my dear, it would be much too dangerous for me to allow a witness to live who knows about all this here." To emphasize his words, he pointed his Colt toward his brother who hadn't moved since he fell to the ground.

"What do you mean?" Elizabeth asked, her face pale and her eyes huge with fear. He saw in her eyes that she understood what he meant. The harmonious world she used to know burst into a thousand shards that cut through her like daggers. The man she loved with all her heart had turned into a dangerous stranger with a weapon in his hand.

Bewildered, she watched her husband raise the blued revolver. He aimed at her heart, but didn't look at her. He directed his gaze at the far end of the cavern where a stranger stood. Nobody had noticed him previously. The man was dressed in black clothes and a black hat with a wide brim that cast a shadow across his face. A knowing smile played across his lips. His eyes were piercing and almost as dark as pieces of polished onyx.

Elizabeth shook like the leaves in a cold autumn breeze. "Please, John, don't do this. I know you love me, and I love you. Aren't we happy with each other? I won't speak a single word to anybody. Trust me. Let's just forget about it and never talk about it again. Let's ride home, John. Please darling, talk to me."

But he stared at her blankly. He cocked the hammer, and the click of it sounded unusually loud.

Elizabeth never saw the dark stranger who stood behind

her. She closed her eyes while tears streamed down her cheeks. Her lips trembled as she struggled to understand what had gotten into her husband. The only thing she was certain of was that she was about to die. She would never see her beloved father again.

Her thoughts were interrupted by the explosion of a loud shot, almost deafening her. Elizabeth waited for the pain, but it didn't come. Confused, she opened her eyes. She saw John's face contorted with pain and hate as he stumbled toward her. A red stain spread on his shirt above his heart.

He tried to raise his gun again as if he still intended to shoot her. He opened his mouth but couldn't speak. Instead, a trickle of blood ran over his lower lip. He crashed to the ground like a felled tree. His eyes stared at the ceiling of the cave but saw no more of this world. John Carson was on his way to hell to pay for his sins.

Elizabeth stood over the body. There he was, her beloved husband with whom she had shared all her dreams. His face was a mask of hate so distorted she barely recognized him. She was heartbroken, having lost her husband twice this day. She lost him when she discovered he had never been the man he pretended to be and knowing that he intended to kill her tore her apart. Then she had lost him forever when he died right in front of her.

"Elizabeth?" She raised her eyes and saw Nate sitting on the ground leaning his upper torso against a rock. He held his left hand pressed against the heavily bleeding wound and his revolver was in his right hand. Smoke drifted from the barrel of the gun.

Nate tried to get back to his feet as Elizabeth walked to him. She avoided looking at John's body and helped Nate stand. He swayed, weak from blood loss, but he was alive. He dropped his gun and held tightly to the woman in front of him.

"Oh, Nate, I'm devastated that John would try to kill me. But you saved me."

Her own beloved husband, the man she had trusted for such a long time had almost shot her. All Nate could do was to hold her tight while she cried like a helpless child. After a while she finally stepped back and rubbed her sleeves over her face.

Urgently, she pulled him by the hand toward the entrance of the cave. "You need the doctor immediately, Nate. Do you think you can ride your horse?" She had to function rationally and get her emotions under control. She was the daughter of an army colonel and had learned her bravery from him.

Nate slowly walked over to the horses. He moaned as he tried to get onto the back of his stallion, but he succeeded in pulling himself into the saddle. Elizabeth rode close by his side to make sure he didn't fall from his horse.

When they passed the trail that led away from the rock cliff, the nickering of another horse alarmed them. But when Elizabeth's mare reacted to it she realized that John's gelding was waiting somewhere close by.

Elizabeth didn't have the heart to leave the poor animal behind, exposed to wild predators and cold weather. She found the gelding tied to a tree and led him behind her mare.

At last, they were on the strenuous path back to town. It was a tough ride for Nate suffering from the gunshot wound. Neither spoke about John whose body still lay in the cave. His stiff hand held the blued Colt, barely covering the serial number that read 666.

CHAPTER EIGHT

***

A NEW BEGINNING

When Nate and Elizabeth arrived in town, she took him straight to the doctor's house. Fortunately, the bullet hadn't caused severe damage as it had been deflected by a rib and went straight through the body without damaging the internal organs. But Nathanial had lost a lot of blood, and the doctor had to perform surgery to stop the bleeding.

Meanwhile, Elizabeth went to her father's house. Colonel Breckenridge was furious when he heard about her ordeal and the events that took place in that cavern. But he embraced his daughter. "My God, I almost lost you, my beloved child." His wrinkled cheeks were wet with tears. The young woman was all the family he had.

For the first time in his life, Breckenridge was sorry his gut feeling about John Carson had been right. The ruthless man had tricked all of them, although his father-in-law had an inkling something wasn't right. Breckenridge felt guilty about not listening to his instinct and doing some research into that good-for-nothing man. John had truly been a wolf in sheep's clothing.

Elizabeth hugged her father, but she stepped back and regarded him seriously. "Father, listen to me. Nathanial shot John. It was the only way to save my life. It was self-defense because John wanted to kill us both. Nathanial got shot but he will survive. He didn't gun down the deputy in his hometown but was mistakenly blamed for it years ago. John was the real murderer of the law man. You have to help Nathanial. Please make sure that he gets a fair trial."

Miles Breckenridge studied his daughter's face for a moment. "I will help him. He saved the most precious thing in my life, didn't he? How could I not obey your wishes? I promise I will try my best to save the young gentleman from the gallows."

***

Colonel Breckenridge kept his promise. When Nathanial had recovered from his gunshot wound, he faced a fair trial in town. Even his mother was brought to court. After all those years Nate was finally able to tell her the truth about the fateful night and the murder of the deputy nine years ago.

A couple of days after the trial, a letter arrived in town. It was written by Nate's father who begged him to come back home.

***

John's body remained in the cave. Nobody volunteered to grant the ruthless murderer a decent, Christian burial.

A few months after the events took place, some Cowboys came into town. They told a tale about their cattle grazing close to the rock cliff. According to them, a strange-looking cowboy threatened them with a gun. When they called him out the man disappeared without a word, and they couldn't find him anywhere. The horsemen claimed that he disappeared like the early fog on a sunny autumn day.

***

Five months after the shooting in the cavern, Nathanial returned to the little ranch in the peaceful valley. Elizabeth was about to carry a basket with wet laundry off her porch. She saw the rider who slowly directed his horse through the gate. His hat was pulled over his face even though the sun stood low on the horizon behind him. She had to shade her eyes and blink a couple of times against the glaring light. At first, she didn't recognize him. Finally, when he was close enough to jump out of the saddle, she realized it was Nathanial Carson.

"Do you need any help with that laundry again, ma'am?" Nate showed her his boyish smile, but his eyes appeared serious.

Elizabeth put down the heavy basket holding the wet clothes and motioned him to the porch. "Nate, what in the world are you doing out here? How is your father?"

"Father passed away. The consumption got the best of him. At least we had enough time to talk things over. It broke his heart when he heard that John tried to kill us both. I wished he had never heard it, but mother told him the truth before I was able to prevent it. She didn't think there should be more secrets standing between the two of us."

"I am so sorry, Nate. I wished you'd had more time with him." Both remained silent for moment, caught up in nightmarish memories. But then Elizabeth smiled warmly. "How about a glass of lemonade?"

He smiled back at her. "Who could ever resist your lemonade?"

She laughed softly and walked into the house while he sat down on the little white bench on her porch. He thought about the day he sat here months ago and the moment he decided to kidnap her.

She will most likely never forgive me for shooting her husband, but I have to ask for her forgiveness. It is the least I can do.

He hadn't seen any other way to rescue her that particular day. It hurt him to talk about it, but he knew that he owed her an apology.

She returned with a tray holding two glasses of cool lemonade and a piece of cake on a plate. He took a glass and the cake, thanked her, but put the glass on the wooden floor. He balanced the cake on his lap.

"Elizabeth, I came here to tell you that I'm very sorry about what happened five months ago. I know you will never forgive me for shooting your husband. But I want you to know that I regret it deeply, and that I'm sorry from the bottom of my heart. I've never seen John act like that. It seemed as if he was a totally different human being when he shot me and aimed that gun at you. I knew he would kill you if I didn't stop him. Father told me that John behaved oddly ever since buying that Colt. But Pa had no clue that John actually shot the deputy with that very same gun."

Elizabeth sat next to him silently studying his sad face. When she finally spoke, her voice was barely more than a whisper. "Nate, it is true that you shot my spouse. But I think what counts more is the fact that you saved my life by doing so. Obviously, I was married to a total stranger. If you hadn't kidnapped me, I still wouldn't know the truth. I lived under the same roof with a brutal murderer. I don't judge you, and I don't blame you because I think you've been punished enough. After all, you have to live for the rest of your life with the burden that you shot your own brother."

He looked over to the corral where the horses were grazing contentedly. For the first time in months, he felt an inner peace. She was right. He would have to live with the fact that he shot his brother, but he also knew that he didn't have any choice. He thanked God that he'd been able to save Elizabeth's life.

She spoke very quietly. "I'm glad that he didn't kill you."

He bent his head toward her as he wasn't sure whether he had understood her correctly. "What did you say?"

She straightened and pulled her shoulders back as if she had to prepare herself for the next words. "I said I'm sure glad that he didn't kill you. And if you want to know the truth, I don't regret that kiss either," she mumbled while her cheeks turned red.

He stared at her speechlessly for a moment and swallowed. "Elizabeth, I…" but she raised her hand to silence him.

"You know Nate, I'm so fed up with behaving according to people's expectations. I'm tired of pretending that I'm Daddy's little girl, the best cook, a loving wife and now a mourning widow. My entire life I adjusted and tried to fit into the given framework. And as the icing on the cake, I was married to a dang liar who wanted to kill me. My God, I'm so sick and tired of it. What about me? When am I allowed to live my own life, the life that I want for myself, Nate?"

She made fists with her hands. He studied her angry face and was surprised at her emotional outburst. He had expected her to perhaps chase him away but not to open her heart to him. She was panting, and her eyes seemed darker than usual. Although her speech surprised him, he understood her well. He had been in the very same situation, being forced to hide his true feelings for years. He knew how dangerous being forced into pretending to be someone else could be. One could easily lose track of one's real identity.

Nate took her glass and set it on the tray along with his own and the plate. He got up and reached out to her, leading her toward the door. She hesitated but eventually followed him.

She stopped in front of the table. When she looked into his eyes, he sensed how nervous she was. Nate touched her cheek softly and she leaned her face against his warm hand. She took a tiny step toward him, and he put his arms around her. He raised her chin and kissed her tenderly.

She answered his kiss passionately and pressed her body against his. His heart hammered against his chest. *God, help me. I've thought about her every single day since I left town.*

She'd put a spell on him, and he sensed that under her soft and well-behaved shell, a female volcano waited to erupt. Obviously, she suppressed the same kind of hunger for life that Nate did himself.

He cleared his throat and seemed short of breath. "Elizabeth, if you want to protect that good reputation of yours then this would be the right moment to send me away. My self-control is limited, especially when you kiss me like that."

She stared into his eyes that had changed into a smoky grey-green shade, giving away his hunger for her. "Show me what passion and burning desire is all about, Nate. Let me feel it the first day of my new life."

That was the instant he lost control. His desire for the woman in his arms broke through like a fierce thunderstorm and he finally gave up battling against his lust.

He easily lifted her off her feet and carried her into the adjoining room where he gently placed her on the bed. Impatiently he pulled his shirt over his head.

Good heavens, this is the very room where my brother slept, he thought with a frown. But it was too late to change the course of destiny or leave. He had to touch her. His feelings for her had grown with each passing week while he was back home. He wanted her in his life for the rest of his days. She had touched his lonely heart like no other woman ever had.

Elisabeth caressed his naked torso with her fingertips. She saw the scar of the gunshot wound and painful memories forced their way into her consciousness. He read it in her eyes and bent down to kiss her demandingly. "Don't think about it, Elizabeth. The only thing that counts right now is here and now, this very moment. This is about you and me. Touch me, darling. I promise you I will make you forget the past."

She touched his stomach muscles and saw the flames of passion burning in his eyes. The way he touched her lit a desire in her body that she had never felt before. She shook with sheer lust and pleasure unknown and new to her. The world outside her bedroom didn't exist. The nightmares of the past vanished into a hidden corner of her subconsciousness. All that counted was Nathanial and his strong arms holding her tight. Elizabeth found herself in his eyes.

Nate tried to hold back his lust to please her but finally he lost the battle against his own arousal. When he was swept away by his hunger for her, Elizabeth felt like the desirable, rebellious woman she always wanted to be.

For the first time in her life, she didn't care what other people thought of her. She lay in the arms of the man who had shot her husband, and only now did she understand what burning desire and seduction felt like.

When dawn painted the sky in soft colors Nate watched Elizabeth sleeping in his arms. The first rays of the morning sun caught in her shiny, copper-colored hair. Smiling, Nathanial Carson finally slept.

***

Many miles north of the ranch a lonely wolf sniffed around the entrance of the small cave. He hunted and his hunger led him to the steep cliff. Suddenly the beautiful animal raised its head and pricked up its ears. Something warned it of danger, and a low growl escaped its throat. The hairs of the wolf's coat bristled around its neck. The wolf turned around and ran downhill, away from the cave as fast as its paws would carry it.

A man in black clothes stood inside the cave. He looked scornfully down at the remains of a man. A gun lay on the ground next to the hand of the skeleton. It appeared to be brand new and clean. The weapon's barrel was blued, and a small serial number was visible. It read "666."

The stranger gazed into the valley below. Some settlers who were new to the area had made camp near the stream that ran at the bottom. Their youngest son prowled the area around the camp on the hunt for rabbits. He wanted to surprise his mother with fresh meat for dinner. As the mysterious man watched the boy walk toward the cave, the stranger smiled. But the smile didn't touch his eyes, darker than a moonless night. Then he vanished like fog on a sunny autumn day. The serial number on the gun disappeared.

When the boy held the gun for the first time later that day, he would read the tiny serial number as 222. The mysterious Colt would have a new owner by sundown…

CHAPTER NINE

***

THE COLLECTOR'S ORDER

Malibu, California July 2020

Michael drove through the posh Malibu neighborhood, searching for the address of his newest client. He enjoyed driving his convertible through the streets on sunny days with the wind blowing through his hair.

Michael Kent was one of the leading experts on antique weapons, especially firearms. People often sought his expertise and judgment about old guns. But this new client seemed to have a different project for him. In any case it promised to be a high-paying job.

Michael or Mike, as some of his friends called him, grew up on a remote ranch in Montana. Since his parents were both faithful Christians, they named him after the Archangel Michael. His mother had always been convinced that Michael would have a special purpose as an adult. She believed that someday he would be tasked with helping others beyond the usual Boy Scout goals.

Michael never knew how she came up with that idea.

He assumed it arose from a motherly instinct. He never questioned it because he knew that she had something that people call the sixth sense.

He smiled when he thought of her. Up to now his most important purpose had been to make enough money to pay the thundering rent on his California apartment and to stay out of trouble. Sometimes he missed the peaceful scenery and solitude of the ranch that lay nestled between a beautiful mountain range and a crystal-clear river. California could be so hectic that one could easily lose all sanity in that crazy state.

"Ah, there it is—twelve Anacaba View Drive," he mumbled. He whistled approvingly. "Boy, oh boy. That is what I call a posh villa."

He parked his car in the wide driveway and walked toward the beautifully carved wooden front door. He noticed the small security camera in the right corner of the eave above his head. A Mexican housekeeper opened the door and Michael introduced himself.

"Good morning, ma'am. My name is Michael Kent. I have an appointment with Mr. Conway."

She nodded and smiled. "Yes, of course. He's expecting you. Would you follow me, please?"

She turned and led him through an impressive entry hall to a wooden double door next to a marble staircase. She knocked softly, and he heard a voice from the other side of the door. "Come on in."

The housekeeper opened the door and stepped discreetly away from it. She pointed into the room and motioned the visitor inside. A lush red carpet swallowed the sound of Michael's steps. The entire wall to his left was dominated by custom-made bookshelves stacked all the way to the high ceiling. A huge window granted an astonishing view into a beautifully designed garden. A gorgeous antique writing desk in front of the window caught Michael's immediate attention.

A man dressed in an elegant three-piece suit got up and walked around the desk. He seemed to be in his mid-fifties. With an elegant gesture, he stretched out his hand to welcome his visitor.

"Good morning, I'm Gorgo Conway. You must be Mr. Kent, right?"

"Yes, sir, that's me. It's a pleasure to meet you."

"I suggest we sit over there at the conference table, Mr. Kent. May I offer you a cup of coffee or anything else?"

Michael nodded.

"Carmelita, please bring us two coffees and a pitcher with sparkling water. After that, make sure that nobody disturbs our meeting."

"Si, Senor."

Michael briefly admired the collection of books in Conway's library. He walked to the conference table and sat down. From what he could tell, it seemed that Conway owned every book that had ever been printed about historical weapons and other historical artifacts.

Michael was impressed. Conway told him a tale or two about how he found some of the books while they waited for Carmelita with their coffee. It didn't take long before the soft knock at the door announced her return.

She entered with the tray, served the beverages professionally, and left the room quietly. Michael took a sip of the strong brew. Surprised, he raised his eyebrows. It was the best coffee he had ever tasted. It possessed a strong, freshly roasted Italian flavor. Michael had developed a true passion for foreign coffee roasts since he moved to California.

"Well, Mr. Conway, what is it exactly that I can do for you?"

Conway smiled. "You don't waste any time, do you?" he said, "I like that in a man. They say that time is money."

Michael savored another sip of his coffee and waited for the man to spill the beans.

"Are you familiar with the history of Tombstone, Arizona, Mr. Kent?"

The visitor placed his cup on the saucer. "Call me Michael if you don't mind."

"All right, Michael then. By the way, your name sounds British. Is your family originally from England?"

"No, not at all. My ancestors are from Germany. I assume that the name was changed during the first years after we immigrated here. If I'm not mistaken, my family originally comes from an area close to the city of Cologne. But to answer your question, yes, I am familiar with the history of Tombstone, but I'm afraid a lot of it was watered down by all those fake Hollywood movies that are as far from history as the moon is from the state of California."

"I couldn't agree more," said Conway. "But the movie they produced in 1993 is actually pretty close to the real events that took place there. Okay, let's get straight to the point. I'm one of the leading collectors of historical, antique firearms in this country. I own some extraordinary specimens that belonged to people with huge influence and importance in the history of the U.S."

"One outstanding revolver is still missing in my collection, and I want to own that fine weapon. It isn't so much about the six-shooter itself but rather the legend that stands behind it."

Michael reached for his coffee cup. "Which Colt are you talking about?"

"I want to possess Johnny Ringo's revolver, Michael."

Kent stared at the man sitting opposite him. For a moment he was speechless. *Is this man pulling my leg? He must be kidding* me.

As if his host could read Michael's thoughts, he suddenly got up, walked over to his desk, and returned with a historical document in his hands. To Michael's astonishment, it appeared to be a death certificate describing a body that was found besides a small river named Turkey Creek.

According to the document, the poor fellow had committed suicide. The doctor's frilly handwriting described the headwound and identified the dead man as no one less than Johnny Ringo. There was a small notation at the bottom of the certificate mentioning that Johnny Ringo's revolver hadn't been found next to the corpse although the weapon would be expected to be present next to a suicide victim.

Michael was flabbergasted. He stared into Conway's face and waited for further explanations. "You can trust me that this is the original death certificate written by the very doctor who was called to the spot where they found Johnny Ringo. Experts have checked the document more than once. Ringo's Colt has been described numerous times in different documents over the years prior to his suicide, especially by witnesses of events that took place in Tombstone.

"We are talking about a Colt manufactured during the early stage of production for the Army. The engraved serial number reads as 222. The gun has a seven-and-a-half-inch long barrel made from blued steel, and the bullets it uses are caliber forty-five. Until the year 1876 this revolver was only produced for the Army and therefore not available for private customers. Knowing that, one can conclude that Johnny Ringo must have either bought or stolen it from a soldier. Considering the low serial number, we know that this specific firearm was produced within the first year of the model's run."

Michael used a bit of Old West slang. "Why does it have to be this smoke pole?"

"Let's put it this way, I admire the legend that stands behind this Peacemaker. I have always been fascinated by the character of Johnny Ringo. I'm not sure if he really committed suicide, though. Please don't misunderstand. I am fully aware that this is a very difficult task, but I know this Peacemaker is somewhere out there. I feel strongly that the gun still exists."

Michael shook his head. "I want to be honest with you, Mr. Conway. I don't really fancy treasure hunts, and I always prefer facts over legends."

It was difficult for Michael to judge if this man was one of those eccentric freaks, or if he was indeed a collector who should be taken seriously. The accumulation of books in this room showed Mr. Conway was an educated man, and the death certificate looked authentic as well. But despite that, Michael was not foolish enough to think that the given task could be easily fulfilled. Most likely it would be next to impossible to find Johnny Ringo's gun.

"Michael, people claim that you're the best when it comes to finding a specific weapon. You're considered the leading expert when it comes to separating the counterfeit from the authentic as far as ancient firearms. Money doesn't matter and I can guarantee you whatever support you need. I do have excellent connections to grant you admission to important institutions and archives. I can assure you that payment will be very generous and far beyond your usual fee. Of course, I will also cover all travel expenses or extra costs you might encounter. I would suggest I hand over all the research documents I've collected so far, and you give it a try."

Michael hesitated with his answer and thought about the offer for a minute or two. He had no doubt that this commission would be one of the best-paying he had ever received so far. Thinking about it, this job would most likely cover his expenses for the rest of the year. He nodded and took his client's hand to seal the deal.

Mr. Conway got up with a broad smile on his face. He walked to the desk, opened a drawer, and came back with a bulging folder and a leather-bound diary.

"These are all documents, notes and newspaper clippings I found during the last fifteen years of research. This diary belonged to a Catholic monk who lived in New Mexico around 1888. According to his notes, he was the one who kept Ringo's gun after the pistolero's suicide. How it got from Tombstone to New Mexico is unknown. However, the weapon seems to have vanished from New Mexico without a trace."

Michael was quite impressed. Fifteen years of research. *Good heavens, this fellow is absolutely determined to find this firearm. I wonder if he is as obsessed as some other collectors are. One could think that he is searching for the holy grail rather than an ordinary pistol.*

Before Michael left the luxury villa, he emphasized once again how difficult, if not impossible, it would be to find that particular Colt, and that he couldn't give a guarantee that the weapon still existed.

Driving back to his apartment took much longer than he expected since he was caught in the middle of rush hour. He stopped at his favorite restaurant and picked up some food to take home. While warming it in his microwave, he opened a bottle of imported Bavarian beer and looked at the notes and the diary on the table in front of him.

He grabbed the remote control of his stereo and played his favorite CD by the rock band Queen. Then he took a hearty bite from the freshly baked bread roll filled with delicious barbecue. *Hmm, this restaurant never disappoints me. The meat and sauce are to-die-for, as usual.*

He had often tried to convince the owner to reveal the recipe of the delicious barbecue sauce to his mother, but the cook never gave it to him. All he could do was to enjoy eating their delicious food. "Oh well, that's a punishment I can live with," he mumbled while he took a sip of the cold Bavarian brew.

After finishing his meal, he placed the plate in the sink and filled his favorite cup with the strong coffee he had brewed while eating. He sat down at his writing desk and flipped through the pile of documents he had received from Conway during their meeting.

"I must be out of my mind to accept this job. Those dang treasure hunters are the worst of all collectors," he mumbled while he took a sip of the hot beverage, burning his tongue.

The notes and documents contained historical letters, official papers of Tombstone trials, and testimonies of witnesses who saw the body of Johnny Ringo in Cochise County, Arizona. A former law man of Tombstone described Ringo's guns after confiscating them as it was prohibited to walk around town armed at that time.

"Hmm, let's see. Okay, so I'm looking for a seven-and-a-half-inch blued Colt with engraved serial number 222. As Conway mentioned, that means it was produced before 1876 in response to the first order put in by the Army. That must have been quite a lucrative job for Samuel Colt. God only knows how many hundreds of those pistols they ordered from him. From experience I would say it was a very efficient firearm. No wonder the boys from the cavalry wanted to have this Peacemaker. But why in the world should this particular gun still exist? This revolver was produced almost one and a half centuries ago. Most likely it has fallen apart by now."

Michael Kent shook his head, feeling frustrated, and emptied his coffee mug. At that moment, the leatherbound diary caught his eye. He had forgotten about it. He examined it and saw a small cross stamped into its leather cover.

CHAPTER TEN

***

PADRE DE LA VEGA

Michael grabbed the little book and carefully removed the string that held it together. It seemed old, and its pages were dog-eared. Some of the pages were yellowed by age. The pages were covered with gothic inscriptions, and the writing inside was surprisingly beautiful. Padre de la Vega used a quill pen and ink to record his thoughts.

"Wow, that diary looks as if it's more than a hundred years old." Michael was curious about the kind of information he would find in it. The first page held the Rule of the Benedictine religious order. *Ora et labora*—pray and work. Below it, Michael read inscribed in Latin, "Padre Alexandro de la Vega, in the year of our Lord 1888."

The firearms expert read on. The first few chapters described how the man of the *Holy Bible* started the missionary in the settlement of Santa Fe in the new territory of New Mexico. He described the hardship he faced but also spoke proudly of his achievements against all odds.

"Land Sake's Alive. What in the world has a Christian

mission to do with the missing gun of some crazy, drunk *pistolero* of the Old West," Michael wondered? As he continued reading, Michael learned that de la Vega's church community welcomed a young family which had settled in the area. Padre de la Vega took a liking to the son in the family. The boy's name was Josef Hernandez. Just like the other members of his family, Josef was a good Christian and supported the Benedictine padre during mass and other church duties. The Padre wrote:

> I really do like that Hernandez boy. I enjoy his company, and he is a good Christian. Nevertheless, I cannot help but worry about him. He seems to be changing. The boy is reserved and hardly speaks to anyone anymore. His behavior changed suddenly, and I am uncertain what could have caused it.

The servant of the church demonstrated in his writing that he was concerned about young Josef's well-being. He described how the boy began neglecting his duties during mass as well as at home. Nobody knew what was wrong with the boy.

> Since his family went camping for a hunting trip in the mountains, he seems to be avoiding me whenever possible. I had high hopes that he would join our religious order of holy Benedictine monks someday, but now it seems as if he no longer cares about the Bible. Oh God, have I failed to teach him how precious your holy words are?

Michael interrupted his reading for a moment, getting up to refill his coffee. Again, he wondered why this diary was of any importance to Mr. Conway. He grabbed a bottle of water, put it next to the coffee cup, and sat down again. He flipped a few pages forward.

A page that was stained and smeared unlike the others caught his attention. The paper looked as if the Padre had cried bitterly while writing the words.

> Oh, what a tragedy, my Lord and Father. Such a cruel destiny. The boy who holds such a special place in my heart and is close to me like my own son will most likely be executed in a few days. I don't see any way out that could save him. They told me to visit him in the prison cell so he can confess his sins. What sins would a sixteen-year-old boy have? Why, oh God, did such a drama unfold in front of our eyes? Why were we not able to avoid this tragedy?

Astonished, Michael turned the page and wondered what this passage was all about. He learned that Josef Hernandez had stormed into his parent's home when he heard his mother scream in pain. There he witnessed his father beating his mother so severely that he feared his father would kill her.

Nobody in the community had any explanation as to what had triggered off the brutality displayed by the family man. Hernandez was known to be a loving father and husband and a humble member of the church community. He had never shown any tendency toward drinking or abusing his wife or children.

When young Josef entered the house and saw what was

going on, he pulled a gun and shot his father three times until the man lay still on the kitchen floor, covered in his own blood. No one in the community knew how the boy got his hands on the Colt which he used to kill his father.

When they arrested the young fellow, the deputy impounded the revolver and locked it in the town sheriff's desk.

> Sheriff Willbury told me it was a fine weapon that looked quite new. It appeared as if the law dog admired that barking iron with its blued barrel. I don't know about such things, but Willbury said that it was a real Army pistol.
>
> "Everybody in town knows that Josef would never have enough money to buy such a revolver, so we all assume he had stolen it somewhere. My Lord in Heaven, help me understand what in the world got into Señor Hernandez, and why in the world did the boy shoot his own father?

Michael leaned back in his chair and shook his head. He was shocked as he thought about Josef, who had barely been a teenager but mature enough to kill his own father. What a tragedy. Had they really hanged the boy?

Carefully Michael turned the next page, and Padre de la Vega's voice spoke to him from the distance of decades.

> Today they held the trial for Josef Hernandez. Just as I feared, they sentenced the poor chap to death by hanging. The young feller didn't say much during the trial. He claims he cannot remember most

of the fateful events. The only thing he recalls is the memory of his father beating his mother mercilessly.

The last thing he remembers is holding the six-shooter, but he cannot recall pulling the trigger. When the judge asked him where he got the gun, he remained silent at first. Finally, he admitted that he found it in a cave next to a man's skeleton.

Poor Josef seemed confused, and I believe that up to now he might not even be aware of the fact that he committed a murder. Lord, do we really have the right to sentence him to death? Shouldn't we consider that it could have been self-defense when he tried to protect his beloved mother?

The Sheriff showed the murder weapon in court. He described the revolver as a Colt Single Action Army 45-caliber with a blued barrel. If I recall it correctly it even had an engraved serial number, 222. I remember that all the men in the room were fascinated by the outstanding craftmanship that had gone into the weapon. Unlike all the others I experienced a strong feeling of dismay or rather disgust and didn't even touch the tragedy-bringing item.

Michael was about to reach for his cup, but his hands stopped midair. "Now wait a minute, isn't that the Colt that I'm looking for? Now I understand why Conway kept this diary and thought it was a document of importance. Not bad, Mr. Conway, not bad at all."

Suddenly Michael was captivated by the story about the weapon and the circumstances described in the diary. He pulled the little book closer and continued reading Padre de la Vega's notes. He forgot about his coffee and didn't even realize that it had become dark outside.

Mike hoped to find clues to where the gun had been stored after the trial. He continued reading.

> The next day our Sheriff sent a message to me claiming that Josef Hernandez wanted to confess his sins before the execution. He begged me to come to his prison cell for a private conversation, and the Sheriff agreed to leave us alone for an hour. I was grateful that he did so. I'm sure the man of the law was fully aware how close Josef is to me. I finished today's chores early, and I was about to go to the prison. My Heavenly Father, I ask for your support to grant me strength to prepare Josef for his death. I hope and pray that I'm able to comfort him.

Michael imagined himself in de la Vega's situation. For a member of the Benedictine order, strict adherence to the Ten Commandments and the Bible was an absolute must. The monk felt devastated trying to follow the laws of God and the laws of the community against the feelings in his own heart. This monk cared for the boy, and he felt helpless because he couldn't save him from the gallows.

Michael wrestled with imagining how helpless the Padre must have felt. If the Padre tried to free Josef, he would have broken the law of the territory as well as God's law. So, he could only try to comfort his friend knowing he would be hanged a few days later.

Michael touched the ageing pages of the diary, "It must have broken his heart to witness young Josef hanging from the gallows," he mumbled. He turned the page and found another entry with the same date as the page before.

> The poor soul confessed his sins. Meeting Josef for the last time in private was very painful for me. Considering that he would lose his young life in three days hurts me deeply. He cried and so did I. But Josef also gave me an order. It was an unusual conversation.
>
> I had to promise him that I would keep the gun which he used to kill his father and to find a safe place for that deadly instrument. Josef urged me to make sure that no man ever laid hands on the Colt again. I asked him if we shouldn't sell the revolver and give the money to his poor mother to support her financially. She would have to manage without her husband and son from now on.
>
> I told him I was quite sure the six-shooter would bring a nice amount on the local market. But Josef would hear nothing about it. Rather, the opposite was the case. He begged me to keep the gun locked in a sacred place such as a church.
>
> At first, I didn't understand why he was so determined, but then he told me that he'd had a powerful dream. He claimed that an angel visited him inside the prison cell, and this messenger of God told him that the

weapon had to be taken to a secure place
by Padre de la Vega.

Oh Lord, I'm not worthy to question
your mysterious ways, and I don't doubt for
a second that you have sent this message
to poor Josef. So, I will make sure that this
terrible weapon remains safely hidden in
your sacred church.

I picked up the Colt at the sheriff's office and told him that we cannot ignore the
last will of a dying man. He finally agreed
to it, but I noticed that it seemed difficult
for him to part with the revolver.

Now the artifact of death is wrapped in
a blessed stole and hidden in a small trunk.
I will be on my way after Josef's execution,
just like I promised the poor fellow.

The next page in the diary described the day of the hanging. It was a short note, but Michael sensed the sadness
between the lines.

With a broken heart I had to attend the
execution of Josef Hernandez today. Sometimes I ask myself why You put such a
heavy burden on my shoulders, my Lord
and Father. Nevertheless, I serve you as
your humble monk and I thank you that
Josef was granted a faster death when the
rope broke his neck. Please have mercy and
welcome the poor chap's soul. Forgive him
the sin he committed and lead my way so
I can do the right thing just as I promised

the boy. Today I can imagine the pain that
you, my Heavenly Father must have felt
when you lost your own son.

Michael got up and quickly went to the bathroom. Then he closed the shades in his living room. It was dark outside, and he was surprised at how fast the afternoon had passed. "What a sad and tragic ending for someone whose life had just begun," he mumbled thoughtfully. He wasn't hungry and decided to skip dinner. Instead, he picked up a cold Coke from his fridge and sat down at his desk again.

Only two pages were left in the diary after Josef's death. Surprisingly, he recorded his return to the monastery in Spain where he came from. The diary ended with a Benedictine hymn which often accompanies the Prayer of Compline, recited the last thing in the evening. Michael knew the hymn well, as his mother had taught him different religious prayers and psalms during the years of his childhood. She had always been convinced of the power of prayer, whether spoken or sung.

> *When the darkest night wraps around us*
> *And dreams and delusions torture us*
> *When we get threatened by doubts and fears*
> *helplessly exposed to the power of evil*
> *Christus, but then you are our life, truth,*
> *and light*
> *You my caring protector stay close to me*
> *so that our faith may shine bright in all of us*
> *during the dark hours of our sleep*
> *The son and the father we are pleading for it*
> *and the Holy Ghost that unites both of them*
> *The Holy Trinity that leads everything in*

> *this worth*
> *shall protect us through this night. Amen.*

Michael Kent felt cold, and he trembled, but he couldn't explain why. He found it strange that de la Vega ended his diary with this specific hymn. It almost seemed as if he feared something. Michael closed the diary and leaned back, holding his cup of tepid coffee in his right hand.

"Okay, so the weapon definitely existed in Santa Fe and the last person known to have owned it is Padre de la Vega. Question is, where did he go with it? Did he take it along when he returned to the monastery in Spain? Josef told him to bring the Colt to a sacred place of God. Hence it would actually make sense to keep it locked in a church or an abbey. I just wonder why the boy claimed that the gun should never be touched by any man again, and why in the world did he call that pistol 'evil?'"

Puzzled, he shook his head and put all the documents and clippings into a pile. He decided to take a shower and call it a day. Tomorrow would be early enough to continue his research, and it would be easier to concentrate after a good night's rest. He had an idea about where he could find some additional information.

Michael went right to sleep, but he had odd nightmares about a teenager of Mexican descent who warned him about the Colt. The boy raised his index finger while wearing a hangman's noose around his neck.

When he got up in the morning and started his coffee maker, he felt as if a truck had run him over. He prepared a bowl of cereal and drank two cups of the strong brew, hoping that he would feel fit enough to continue the research about Johnny Ringo's gun. He arranged his pens, coffee, and the material he got from Mr. Conway on his desk and started to work.

CHAPTER ELEVEN

***

FREDERICKSBURG, TEXAS

As he sat at his desk with the archives, a newspaper clipping yellowed with age caught his attention. The headline sounded promising: "Heritage of Legendary Weaponsmith Found in Old Archives of Famous Colt Firearms Manufacturing in Connecticut."

Michael checked the date of the article. It was printed in 2004. Michael couldn't help but feel as if he had been jumping back and forth between centuries during his search for that famous Peacemaker. The collected documents covered over one hundred-forty years from pioneer times to today. He read the article.

During renovation work inside the administration building of the Colt Firearms Manufacturing in Hartford, Connecticut, construction workers found a small, secret chamber hidden behind one of the old walls. The small room held a work desk and a wooden cabinet filled with old documents such as technical drawings, sales accounts, and designs for firearms that were never built. Included among the papers were lists containing serial numbers of the first weapons delivered to the government and the army.

The Colt management is considering manufacturing a few guns based on the antique plans. These limited-edition replicas would be sold to collectors as part of the celebration for their upcoming company jubilee.

A small bed and a diary that belonged to an early employee named Ludwig Schmied were also found in the little room. Mr. Schmied was of German heritage and, according to the documents, hired as a gunsmith.

Michael took one of his favorite chocolate cookies from the big jar which always stood at the corner of his desk. His mother baked them and sent them regularly to his California home. She knew how much he savored them. So far, his sweet tooth hadn't affected his athletic build.

According to the newspaper clipping, Colt Firearms Manufacturing had located a distant relative of the Colt gunsmith named Schmied. It was an elderly woman in her late sixties who lived in the formerly German settlement called Fredericksburg in Texas.

Mr. Colt sent her the diary of Ludwig Schmied in a beautifully engraved wooden

box. Colt Firearms Manufacturing emphasized how much Frieda Miller's relative
was responsible for the early success of
the company by honoring him in a framed
certificate. According to archive documents, he was the design engineer for the
legendary army Colt Peacemaker.

Frieda Miller, whose maiden name is
also Schmied, the same as Ludwig's sur-
name, commented rather reluctantly. With
a charming German accent, she astonished
our reporter by saying that it would be better if the past was left alone. She did not
respond to further inquiries.

However, the management of Colt
Firearms Manufacturing is thrilled about
the unexpected discovery, as it offers the
opportunity to research the development of
different models at the early stages of the
company's history.

"Wow, I'll be darned. Maybe I should try to call the old lady
and ask her if she found anything of interest in Ludwig's
notes. Don't know if it might lead me somewhere but it's
sure worth a try," he mumbled to the empty living room.

His growling stomach made him glance at the clock
on the corner of the desk. To his surprise, it was already
noon and high time to order food. He called his favorite
Thai restaurant just around the corner from his apartment
and ordered his favorite prawn curry. Then he turned on
the TV to watch the news and stock market report. As they
ended, the doorbell rang.

He opened the door and welcomed his friend Chang

who delivered the food prepared by his mother in the small restaurant called Bangkok Treasures. "Hello, Chang. How are you doing? How's business?"

"Everything is good. We're doing alright. We got two boxes of fresh mangos today. Mom sent you one. She still claims that you don't eat enough fresh fruit. You know how she is."

Michael laughed, accepting the bag containing the food. "Here you go. Here's your money, Chang. Please give my regards to your parents. Thank your Mom for the extra-large portion of fried rice and the mango. The dish smells wonderful as usual."

"We would be delighted to welcome you at the restaurant some time. You work too much, Mike. You need to get out more."

Michael held up a finger. "Tell me something new, Chang. Looks like I caught the Californian workaholic virus . Sometimes I wonder if I should have stayed back home at the ranch for a more peaceful life."

Chang laughed at that, then he patted Mike on the shoulder, turned, and left.

Michael walked over to the sideboard and arranged his food on a plate. Despite being single, he never fancied eating straight out of the restaurant containers like many of his friends did. He viewed it as a matter of cultural refinement to serve good food in a tasteful way and appreciate it properly.

As usual, the prawn curry was delicious, with exactly the right amount of chili and garlic. After finishing his meal, he put the dishes into the dishwasher and returned to his desk.

The weapons expert jotted down the most important facts from de la Vega's diary and took notes from the pile of paper clippings so he could more easily analyze the facts. His goal was to figure out a strategy for how and where to search for the famous gun. After working for what seemed a short time, darkness surprised him for the second day in a row. This case absorbed his attention, and he lost track of time and place as he worked on it. Reluctantly, he called it a day.

Usually, Michael Kent slept dreamlessly and well, but nightmares harassed his sleep for the past two nights. A ghostly Johnny Ringo pursued him as he slept. Again, and again, the notorious outlaw of Tombstone's past pointed to the tiny, bleeding wound in his temple.

His phone rang at 6:30 a.m., startling him awake. Michael almost dropped the mobile to the floor when he yanked it off his nightstand. "Hello," his hoarse voice grumbled into the phone. He felt terrible, as if he'd been run over by a truck, like he hadn't slept at all.

"Good Morning, Mr. Kent. It's me, Gorgo Conway. Have you gone through the documents already?" Michael sat up in bed and glanced over at his alarm, scowling at the clockface.

"Mr. Conway, it is 6:30 in the morning—not the ideal time for a business conversation, if you ask me. But to answer your question, yes, I went through all your research material and will follow up on a few clues today."

Mr. Conway ignored Michael's complaint about the early hour and asked the expert to keep him up to date. When Michael thought about it later, he decided it sounded like a command to send him a daily report.

Michael Kent didn't know why, but he had disliked his client from the first minute they met. There was something about this eccentric collector that appeared unearthly. His black clothes added to that impression.

What the hell, since I am awake already, I might as

well go down to Ruth's Café and enjoy breakfast with gallons of her robust coffee. Looks like an early start to some extra hours of work.

Michael maintained his grouchy mood after having been awoken in such rude manner. Ruth welcomed him with her typical broad smile. She was the owner of the tiny coffee shop on the corner. He couldn't recall ever having seen her when she wasn't cheerful or welcoming her customers with a smile.

"Howdy, handsome. How are you doing today?"

He sat at the bar and pulled the coffee she had already poured closer. "Hey, Ruth. Well, I feel very tired. It was a rough night."

"How come? What's the matter?"

"I'm working a new project. Quite a hard nut to crack … and the client is a real weirdo. He called me this morning at 6:30 a.m., would you believe?"

"My, oh, my, obviously the fellow doesn't know that you are real grumpy in the early mornings. Okay, in that case, I'll prepare my famous Spanish omelet for you and add two Polish smoked sausages. I promise that'll get you back onto your feet in the blink of an eye."

Smiling, Mike slapped the counter. "That would be wonderful, Ruth. You really know how to make a man happy." She laughed and walked over to her kitchen. It wasn't long before she placed a loaded plate in front of Michael. The aroma of spicy eggs and fat, dripping sausages made his mouth water.

Ruth refilled his coffee cup and watched him eat with an amused twinkle in her eye. He shoveled the food into his mouth as if he'd never tasted anything so good.

Ruth had been a great friend right from the first day they met in the small café. She always had an open ear for him to unload his sorrows or problems with work. Sometimes he pulled her leg by calling her "Mom," teasing her for being constantly concerned about his well-being. Not only was Ruth a wonderful cook, but also a truly good soul.

When he had cleaned his plate, he pushed it across the bar, grinning boyishly. "Would you be so kind as to roll me back to my apartment? I ate so much that I'm not even sure I can lift myself off this barstool."

"Oh, quit talking nonsense, young man. You are slim and athletic and can probably run up the stairs to your apartment."

He winked at her, paid for his breakfast, and waved goodbye to her as she walked over to some new customers.

When Michael arrived back at his apartment, he was still annoyed about the early call from his client, but the tasty breakfast and freely flowing coffee had helped lift his mood.

He sat down at his work desk and got started. It took quite a while, but finally he found a phone number for Mrs. Frieda Miller in Fredericksburg, Texas. Straight away he dialed the number and hoped that the lady still lived at the same address. By now she must be in her early seventies.

The phone rang a couple of times, and Michael was about to hang up when a firm voice finally answered.

"Hello?"

"Good morning, Mrs. Miller. My name is Michael Kent. I'm sorry for disturbing you. I'm calling you because of some research I'm doing for Colt Firearms Manufacturing."

He had decided to use a white lie as he was quite certain that she might mistake him for a promotional caller and would hang up on him. At least the Colt company was not unknown to her.

"I see, and what can I do for you?"

"I'm doing some research about a former Colt series project. It would be very helpful if you allowed me to take a look at the diary of Ludwig Schmied. Management informed me that it belongs to you now."

Her faint German accent still lingered. "That is correct. Don't get me wrong, young man, but I would like to know what this is all about. Ludwig was the son of a great-grand-uncle—a distant relative. My family has suffered more than enough hardship because of the Colt 45. You surely understand that I do not wish his memory to be soiled or used in a questionable context."

"Yes ma'am. I understand you very well, Mrs. Miller. I can assure you that I want to praise his talent and keep his reputation unharmed. I'm an expert in antique firearms currently working on a research project about the earliest models of a specific army Colt that your relative Ludwig Schmied developed and constructed."

"I guess I can agree to giving you access. But I have to admit that the diary contains many pages. Too many to go through on the phone. It doesn't make sense to read them to you, and I don't really know what kind of information you seek from the pages written by that young man with such a tragic story. I want to be honest with you, Mr. Kent. I would prefer to get to know you in person and show you the diary when we meet face to face. I don't want to send it by mail to a complete stranger. As I mentioned before, our family has had its share of drama. Destiny hasn't always been merciful to the Schmied family."

To further reassure the skittish diary-owner, Michael said, "I'm sorry to hear that ma'am. I can see why you'd be careful."

"I'm sure you're aware that I live in Fredericksburg, Texas. According to your area code, you must be some-where in California, which means you would have to travel to my town."

"I'm sure I can arrange that. I'll check on the connecting flights and call you back to let you know my travel dates. I hope that will be okay for you."

"Of course, Mr. Kent. I'm retired and have few obligations. I can adjust to the dates that would be best for you. I rarely receive visitors and meeting you would be quite nice for change. The only thing I'm asking from you is that you treat the history of my family with respect."

Michael promised her again that he wouldn't use any of the information without her approval. After confirming their next steps, he hung up.

Then he called Mr. Conway, who picked up on the first ring. "Mr. Conway, I'm going to Fredericksburg, Texas to meet with Frieda Miller and review the diary of Ludwig Schmied."

Michael could hear Conway's exuberance through the phone. "Excellent. The most logical next step. Don't worry about your travel expenses. I'll transfer the necessary amount to your account within the next hour. Two grand should cover it."

However, Conway didn't seem convinced that Mrs. Miller would be able to provide new information. "Originally, I offered the Colt company quite a high amount for the diary, but it was too late, as they had already sent it to the old lady. I'm not sure if it can really help us find Johnny Ringo's gun. That's why I didn't follow that lead. That Ludwig Schmied fellow was just a gunsmith for the Peacemaker series. Or he most likely was the designer who worked on the original drawings. How likely do you think it is that you can find the whereabouts of the weapon from that diary?"

Michael clicked his tongue. "I don't have a clue if I'll find further hints about that gun in Ludwig's notes. But we have no idea where that six-shooter ended up after the events that took place in Santa Fe. I'd rather follow one trail too many, than overlook something that might show us where to look next. But I'll pursue it only if you wish me to do so."

"Of course, Mr. Kent, go ahead. Like I told you before, money isn't an issue. I'm quite sure that we will have to follow the tracks left by Padre de la Vega. Sadly, I have to admit that I'm not on the best of terms with the Catholic Church. They don't grant me access to certain institutions or archives. Maybe it's jealousy of my wealth or the rather uncomfortable research I did regarding certain artifacts in the past. So, I'm glad to have you on my team taking care of that. Please keep me informed and let me know when you're back from Fredericksburg."

Michael agreed to that. He was quite sure that discovering where Padre de la Vega spent his last years after returning from his missionary work in Santa Fe would provide missing pieces. Michael's gut feeling told him that the Benedictine monk kept the revolver close to him.

Less than thirty minutes after the call, the promised two thousand dollars had been transferred to Michael's account. The young man was quite surprised by Mr. Conway's generosity.

Michael could tell that Conway didn't really believe the handwritten diary concealed precious information. Neither did his employer discourage him from making the trip. Perhaps he thought a new set of eyes could reveal new truths.

It was early afternoon when Michael Kent booked his Southwest Airlines flight from Los Angeles to San Antonio, Texas. He would cover the remaining seventy miles to Fredericksburg with a rental car he had booked online the same time as his flight.

Michael had more than enough time to pack a bag and prepare for the meeting with Frieda Miller before his flight two days later. Although he was able to check in online, the journey would still take about six hours, so he decided to book a nice resort hotel and stay overnight in Fredericksburg.

It was a beautiful city that had kept much of its German heritage and culture alive. Michael was looking forward to enjoying some German food and a cold, imported Bavarian beer after his meeting with Frieda. Following a night in a resort, his return flight would bring him back to bustling Los Angeles, unless he decided to stay an additional night.

Later that evening the firearms expert called Frieda Miller once again and asked her if the flight he had booked in two days would suit her schedule. She told him that she had no better plans and that she would welcome him. She also recommended a lovely German restaurant for his dinner in town. "One thing is for sure—the Germans always think practically and ahead of time," he laughed into his empty living room.

The following day he packed what he needed for the two-day trip. Since he had to be at the airport before 7:00 a.m. he planned to go to bed quite early. He spent the afternoon paying a visit to the Thai restaurant Chang's parents owned, where he enjoyed one of their delicious coconut-milk simmered dishes.

While he relished the tasty food, a sudden idea came to his mind. Unlike his client, Mr. Conway, Michael had a good connection in the Roman Catholic Church. He remembered that one of his cousins was a monk in one of the European monasteries. If he wasn't mistaken, Alexander was a member of the Benedictine order, just as de la Vega had been.

Michael wondered if the Benedictines kept records about members of the order. If that was the case, chances were quite good that he could discover something about Padre de la Vega's life after he left Santa Fe.

When Michael returned to his apartment, he decided to call his mother in Montana. She was happy to hear from her son and asked him how he was doing. Then she asked which new project was keeping him too busy to visit them. Michael's mom was a faithful Christian who believed firmly in pacifism and "turn the other cheek." He knew that she wasn't enthusiastic about his choice to become an expert in firearms. Therefore, he never told her much about the contracts he accepted.

Michael directed the conversation to his cousin and explained that he needed information from the Benedictine order for specific research he was doing.

"Oh, Michael, I don't think the monks know anything about deadly weapons. You know that they live a peaceful life according to the rules of the Bible. Their main credo is *ora et labora* — 'pray and work.'"

"I know, Mom, but I'm trying to find out more about a specific padre who was a missionary in New Mexico over a hundred years ago. I believe that brother Alexander might be able to help me access the records of their abbey. I am quite certain they have information I need in those archives."

"Okay, hold the line. I'll get my address book. If I remember correctly, Alexander was transferred to another abbey. I wrote a letter to him not long ago. Just give me a minute."

Michael heard his mother's steps moving away from the phone, and he imagined her walking across the kitchen to her little desk. He knew every room by heart in that house and was suddenly aware of how much he missed the peaceful home in the enchanting mountains of Montana.

Her steps moving closer interrupted his thoughts, and she picked up the phone. "Hey Michael, are you still there?"

"Of course. Got the address?"

"Okay, let's see." He heard her flipping the pages of her address book. "Brother Alexander was in an abbey in France at first. Wonderful building. I googled it sometime back and marveled at the pictures. Unfortunately, there weren't enough monks left to keep the Abbey of Mont-Saint-Michel maintained. Now it is a UNESCO world heritage site and is managed by the National monuments center of France. Well, much better than to let it fall apart, right? Do you have a pen to write this down?"

Michael's mother sometimes took longer than his patience allowed. He tapped the pen on the paper. "Yep, I'm ready, Mom."

"The address is Brother Alexander Slater, Monastery Einsiedeln, in 8840 Einsiedeln, Switzerland."

"Wow, so he lives in beautiful Switzerland now, right in the center of Europe, is it?"

"Oh Michael, don't you know that we have relatives all over Germany, Switzerland and even southern England? I do believe that almost every American has ancestors and relatives all over the world. Well, maybe except the American natives, of course. They are truly American."

"If that ain't the truth, Mom. I'm sorry, but I have to keep this call short. I'm going to the airport very early tomorrow morning, and I better get some sleep. Please give a hug to Pa and remind him not to work too hard. Don't forget, you've got the ranch boys for that. Thanks once again for your help."

"You're very welcome, Michael. I hope you get to visit us soon. We're missing you up here in big sky Montana. Please be careful while you travel and remember to eat regularly, my son."

"Yes Ma'am. I'll visit you for Thanksgiving at the latest, but if things go right, hopefully earlier. I'm planning on a full week's vacation this summer. I want to go fly fishing with Dad like we used to when I was a teenager. I'll let you know when I'm back. Talk to you later."

Although he was happy with his life in California, he always missed his parents and knew they felt the same. Michael was their only child. He planned to return to Montana as soon as he had saved up enough money to build his own home. He wanted to increase his reputation as one of the leading experts for antique weapons in the United States. Then he could work from Montana and cut down on traveling so much. He felt like the time was right to consider settling down for good.

Michael decided to get in touch with his cousin, Alexander. He wanted to find out if Alexander could grant him access to the archives of the Benedictine monastery in Switzerland. Unfortunately, he couldn't call now due to the time difference. Switzerland was eight hours ahead and it was the middle of the night there, so he had to postpone calling his relative until he returned from Texas. Maybe he would gather more information in Texas that would make his research in the Benedictine archives easier, if the monks granted him access.

With a smile Michael recalled his youth when he and Alexander spent a lot of time together. They were careless teenagers who experienced many adventures together. He remembered the countless fishing trips and caves explorations close to his parents' ranch.

However, Alexander heard the call of God quite early, and after years of helping the local priest in church he entered a monastery.

It was a shock for Michael when Alexander told him that he planned to become a monk but now, years later, he understood that a person cannot escape their destiny.

Michael knew that the order of Saint Benedict had collected an enormous amount of knowledge and wisdom in the form of old documents, countless books, artifacts, and antiques. Their monasteries were unbelievable sources of art treasures and records that could increase a collector's heartbeat in the wink of an eye.

Nowadays life in the monastery was not as shielded as it had been centuries ago, and monks all over the world contributed their share to charity work and developing communities.

Considering his talent for languages it was not surprising that Alexander relocated across the ocean to the so-called "Old World," and ended up in a monastery which could look back on a thousand years of history.

If Michael remembered correctly, Brother Alexander spoke German, French, and Italian fluently. He hadn't forgotten his English mother tongue, and most likely he knew a great deal of Latin, as the Benedictines recited their prayers in that dead language. Alexander's ability to speak several languages must be a helpful enrichment for the internationally known Swiss monastery. The one thing that Michael and Alexander had in common was their immense hunger to constantly increase their scope of knowledge.

CHAPTER TWELVE

***

THE DIARY OF LUDWIG SCHMIED

It was time to catch some sleep, as the following day would be a long and strenuous one. Michael hit the road by 6:30 a.m. on his way to the airport. As he had been countless times before, he was astonished by the number of cars on the city's freeways.

For Michael, this was an ungodly time to be out and about. It was unbelievable that hundreds of thousands of cars were already rushing to some unknown destination. In less than an hour, the roads all over the city and surrounding areas would be at a standstill.

Michael was relieved when he entered the departure area of the Los Angeles International Airport. Since he had checked in online the previous evening and carried only hand luggage, he had enough time left to enjoy breakfast along with two cups of coffee. After breakfast, he strolled to the departure gate.

Michael tried to relax during the flight to San Antonio. Since he didn't know what Ludwig Schmied's diary was all about, he couldn't prepare specific questions for Frieda Miller. He had to wait until he met the lady.

Try to see it positively. This is your chance to get out of Los Angeles for a little while. It's almost like a short vacation even if it's just for two days. Michael had a strong feeling that this job would keep him quite busy for the next couple of weeks.

After the plane had touched down in San Antonio, he walked straight to the rental car counter, filled in the paperwork, and went to the parking deck to pick up his car. Less than thirty minutes after landing in Texas he was on his way, taking the highway that led to Fredericksburg.

He would have loved to explore the city of San Antonio if he had two more days to hang around. San Antonio was an interesting melting pot of different cultures each of which had left their trace in the architecture and cuisine.

A riverwalk led through the art and restaurant quarter along the San Antonio River, past the Alamo and colonial Spanish mansions. Boats floated up and down the river beside the pedestrian traffic and added to the picturesque appearance of San Antonio.

Michael planned to return to this amazing city for one of his future vacations. He liked very much what he had seen from above during the plane's descent.

After an hour of unhurried driving, Michael arrived in the town of Fredericksburg. The town lay nestled in the Texas hills right in the center of the famous vineyards of the Lone Star State.

Michael whistled admiringly through his teeth at the spectacular scenery. Both sides of the road were framed by well-kept vineyards and meadows covered in wildflowers. Never in his life had the young man seen such colorful carpets of blooming red poppies and wild lupins.

Now he was really looking forward to the two days in Fredericksburg. He spontaneously decided to postpone his return flight for a day.

"Why not? I can work from everywhere, thanks to my computer." Being self-employed sure has its advantages. He was able to organize his working hours as he wished.

Using the GPS, he found the small, well-kept house that belonged to Frieda Miller right away. Her home was a picture- perfect copy of a Hallmark card scene. The beautiful garden was surrounded by a freshly painted, white picket fence. Rows and arrangements of blooming flowers attracted uncounted numbers of butterflies and bees.

Michael parked his car next to the walkway and strolled toward the garden gate. He inhaled the scent of the blooming flowers and closed his eyes to hear the humming of the busy insects in the air.

He imagined the seventy-year-old Frieda Miller to be a bit on the weak side and maybe even using a walker. He was quite surprised when she opened the door before he stepped onto the porch. Behind her the house beamed a cozy, welcoming atmosphere that reminded him of his parent's home in Montana.

Just like his mom, Frieda Miller owned a front porch swing that invited guests to sit down on the colorful pillows for a relaxed conversation. The pillars that supported the wooden patio reminded him of Victorian craftmanship.

Frieda Miller was the opposite of the person he had expected her to be. A tall and slim woman with a tanned, pleasant face stood before him. She wore tight fitting denim jeans, and her hair was cut in a perfectly styled bob.

Her garden was so well-groomed that he assumed she must work in it regularly. Michael was sure that she once had been a very beautiful woman. Even now, in her seventies she was still attractive and carried herself proudly. She greeted him warmly, and her voice had a husky tone to it.

"Mr. Kent? Mr. Michael Kent?"

"Yes, ma'am. That's me. I am sincerely thankful that you made this meeting possible."

But she just laughed. "Mr. Kent, it doesn't happen very often that an old lady receives visitors from sophisticated California. Here in Fredericksburg everything is a bit laid back, as you can imagine. To be honest, your visit is a nice change from my daily routine. Life can be rather boring when you live alone."

"Come on in. Make yourself comfortable. I prepared homemade lemonade and a pot of fresh coffee, as well. All Germans are addicted to coffee. I think we could beat the Californians easily when it comes to that," she added with hearty laughter.

Michael followed her into the house and smiled. He liked the lady from the very first minute. He thought it was rather amusing that she still considered herself a German even though she was most likely born in the United States. But of course, he couldn't tell that for sure.

The house was small, but it radiated a storybook coziness. The small country kitchen was laid out in an open concept with direct access to the bright living room. The rooms weren't overfilled, as was often the case in houses of elderly folks. Her furniture spoke of a sophisticated taste. The wall behind the couch was entirely covered by bookshelves. *Ah, Mrs. Miller is a lady of education,* he thought admiringly.

She pointed to a chair and told him to make himself comfortable. In only a couple of minutes, the lemonade and two crystal glasses stood in front of him. A pot of coffee was added next, exuding a wonderful aroma. "I have a weakness for foreign roasts," she admitted, grinning and looking at the floor. "The Italian coffees especially got me hooked. They surely make the best coffee in the world."

Michael couldn't help but laugh. "I think we have something in common. My orders for foreign imported coffee beans in general and Italian specifically are slowly but surely busting my budget."

Michael was convinced that his visit here in Texas would be well worth it, as Frieda Miller had a refreshing personality. They clicked from the very beginning.

"How was your trip? Did you have a pleasant flight?"

Michael nodded. "It was okay. I just don't like hanging around at airports for too long. Too many people, if you know what I mean."

"Well, Mr. Kent, I assume you didn't eat well on your flight to San Antonio, did you? I know that nobody wins a flower bouquet with the food they serve on those flights."

Michael laughed as he knew that saying well from his mother. *Seems to be a typical German expression,* he thought.

"Please call me Michael."

"I'd gladly do that, but only if you call me Frieda from now on. I feel so terribly old when someone addresses me so formally."

Michael knew that his mother would feel the same way. He confirmed that the sandwich served on the flight hadn't looked appealing, and he was glad he'd eaten a decent breakfast at the airport.

Frieda got up, opened the 'fridge, and turned around with a big plate in her hands. At first Michael looked at her in astonishment, and then his entire face lit up when he realized that she was about to serve him a Black Forest cake with cherries on it.

"Oh… my goodness. Is that an original homemade Black Forest cherry cake?" She nodded and placed the delicious specialty on the table. The cake looked very mouthwatering. She must have put a lot of work into it.

"Frieda, how could you know that this is my absolute favorite cake?"

"Let's say I have a sixth sense." She cut the gateau and placed a generous piece onto Michael's porcelain plate decorated with a delicate flower design. The moist cake glistened in three layers of dark chocolate and was generously filled with whipped cream and cherries.

Michael waited until she served herself a piece and sat down again. After she poured him a cup of coffee, he brought the first bite to his mouth. The aromas as the bite approached his face were tantalizing. He noticed the smell of cherry schnapps. Into his mouth it went.

He rolled his eyes and rubbed his tummy like a little boy who had just been served his favorite meal. Frieda laughed out loud and asked him to tell her something about himself.

She wanted to know where he came from and what he did for a living. He knew she was trying to figure out his background so she could get a clearer picture of him as a person.

The mood between the two of them was relaxed now. He would have considered it rude to ask her straight away about the diary. He was pretty sure that she would get to that point soon enough.

After a while Frieda got up and walked over to the bookshelves. She returned with a wooden box in her hands and put it on the table in front of him. The lid displayed the beautifully engraved symbol of the Colt Firearms Manufacturing.

She carefully put the cake back into the fridge, refilled

his glass of lemonade and finally looked at him with a serious expression on her face. "Michael, there are certain things that you should know before you take a look at the diary. Ludwig was the younger of two sons, and although he was an extremely talented and successful man, his father always treasured his older son much more."

Frieda paused to take a seat opposite him. "I got to know quite a lot of sad details from stories passed from one family member to the next. Ludwig's father, as well as his older brother, constantly expressed their opinion that Ludwig was not worthy of being a member of their family. So naturally he was a quiet and shy person with a lack of self-confidence."

Michael nodded, wondering where the story about Ludwig Schmied was going, but not wanting to interrupt.

Frieda went on. "My great-granduncle was a wealthy man, and when the time came to split the inheritance between the two sons, Ludwig's father and his elder brother betrayed the young fellow terribly. Not only did Ludwig's brother lay hands on the entire estate but also made sure that poor Ludwig was thrown out of the house."

"The family peace had been disturbed for quite a while and kicking the poor fellow out of his home was no less but the final heartbreaking piece."

Frieda folded her hands in her lap and studied them for a moment. Looking up at Michael, she continued the tragic story. "You can surely imagine that he was not only devastated but also developed a great deal of hate against his own family. As far as I know, he didn't have anywhere he could go next. Fortunately, he found a job at Colt Firearms Manufacturing.

"When the company contacted me about the hidden chamber and the diary, I was wondering if poor Ludwig even lived and slept in that room. Sadly, that was confirmed by them."

Frieda stood up and poured a coffee refill into Michael's cup. She glanced at him but said no more for a few minutes. After asking her permission Michael wrote some notes in his notebook. After a while, she continued to tell her story.

"Ludwig started to work at that company. They must have really been happy with his craftmanship because at the beginning of his notes he mentions that he was entrusted with important orders."

Frieda pointed at the box on the table in front of Michael. "When you read the diary, you will quickly realize that he never overcame the hurt and disappointment his father and brother had caused. I'm sure he loved both deeply and could not understand why in the world they betrayed him the way they did."

Dropping her hand and shrugging, Frieda shared her beliefs about her relative based on what she had read in the book. "Ludwig doesn't write openly about his feelings, but you can read between the lines. I do believe it was uncommon in those days for a man to keep a diary. The last two pages seem rather odd, and although I have read them three times, I still don't know what to make of them. You might be luckier since you know about weapons and being a man and such. However, the tragedy that took place a few days later is not mentioned at all in the diary."

"What tragedy are you talking about?" Michael wanted to know. The story sounded rather intriguing.

Frieda looked through the window into the garden and remained silent. Michael wondered if he had been too indiscreet to fire the question bluntly into her face. When she turned her face toward him, she looked rather sad and continued to tell the tale. "Ludwig's hate against his family must have increased from day to day. I assume that it might have been tempting for him working manufacturing firearms on a daily base. One day he returned to his parent's house. He knew that nobody besides his mother would welcome him there. But those days she didn't have much to say. As you surely know, those were times when women didn't speak out against their husbands or their eldest sons."

Frieda stared out the window into the darkness for a moment before she continued. "That fateful day Ludwig didn't go home to set the record straight or to beg permission to return to the arms of his family. He wanted revenge and pulled a revolver. He shot his father in cold blood. When his brother returned from the stables, he was shocked to find his father lying dead on the floor of his study. But Ludwig wasn't done as his hate against his own brother was even worse. He saw Leopold as most likely responsible for the betrayal. Ludwig raised the Colt a second time and shot his brother in the face, literally destroying the man's skull."

Frieda rested her elbow on the arm of her chair and her cheek on her hand. "My parents told me that Ludwig's mother screamed like a lunatic and ran into her husband's study. Ludwig promised not to harm her but ordered her to leave the room immediately. He led her out of the room and locked the door behind her. The desperate woman heard a third shot and ran out into the street screaming for help."

Michael was speechless. He simply didn't know what to say. Even in his wildest dreams, he wouldn't have expected such a heartbreaking tragedy. No wonder Frieda was so reluctant to share information about her family. Was it possible that the maker of one of the most important historical firearms was a coldblooded murderer?

Can the poor chap be fairly judged for that crime? I don't even know how I would react if such an injustice were to happen to me. Times were different in those days, much tougher. I think Frieda is right about it being tempting to handle guns every day while being stuck in such an unhappy situation.

"Good heavens, Frieda. How terrible. I admit I never would have imagined that. Now I understand why you are so hesitant to show that diary to anyone. What happened after Ludwig's mother ran out of the house?"

She looked down at her wrinkled hands and said, "A few men from the neighborhood ran into the house and broke down the door to the study. Not only did they find Mr. Schmied, Senior and his eldest son lying dead on the floor, but they also found Ludwig sitting behind his father's desk with a bullet hole in his temple. Apparently, he had committed suicide by shooting himself with the same Colt that had executed his family members. The poor devil must have lost his mind. His two victims were buried after a procession through town and a solemn funeral in the family's mausoleum. But Ludwig was more or less dumped outside the cemetery walls in unhallowed ground. One could say he was buried like a rabid dog."

She shook her head. "People were quick to judge him, but to a certain degree I understand what he did. Now don't get me wrong, Michael. Ludwig committed a terrible crime, and murder is never a solution, but we also need to understand that someone with a broken heart hardly ever reacts rationally. I'm quite certain that he felt rejected enough to lose his mind. I assume that the only logical outcome he could think of was a vendetta against those two men who destroyed his life on purpose."

Michael remained silent. This was an unbelievable story, and it surely was hard to digest. Frieda rose and crossed to the table where the wooden chest sat. She opened it and removed the small diary. It was a simple book, bound in black leather, its pages yellowed by age.

Frieda looked into his eyes. "Michael, you told me that you 're going to stay overnight here in Fredericksburg. I've only known you for a couple of hours but I'm sure that I can trust you. Generally, I have good horse sense. Therefore, I want to lend you the diary until tomorrow at noon. That way you can take your time to read it undisturbed in your hotel room and write down all the notes you may need for your research."

"I don't know if it will help you for your project because if I understood you correctly, you're seeking information about the gun that Ludwig constructed. But who knows, you might find some helpful facts in here. I only ask you not to spread anything about this tragedy in public, please. I'm sure you understand that my family has suffered from that murder case for long time."

Michael was surprised by her generosity and thanked her. He assured her that he would return the diary the following day around noontime.

"Frieda, I'd love to pick you up and take you out to lunch as a treat for all the help you've had given me."

"Michael, I'm delighted to accept."

It was already early evening, and Michael bid Frieda farewell as he still had to search for his hotel and check in. It had been a long day and he felt exhausted.

The elderly lady walked outside with him but remained standing on the porch. He put the diary on the passenger seat and typed the address of the Barons Creekside Cabin Hotel into his GPS. Since his client paid him well, he pampered himself with a room in a rustic boutique hotel that lay nestled next to a man-made lake. He waved at Frieda, started the engine, and drove off toward his final destination of the day.

When he arrived at the small hotel, he was rather surprised. The guest rooms were situated in log cabin-style buildings. An artfully designed garden added to the cozy atmosphere. Although the hotel gave off a rustic aura from the outside, the rooms and lobby were designed in a clever mixture between relaxed ranch-style and the amenities of a modern five-star hotel.

He was pleased to have decided on this accommodation and spontaneously changed his reservation from one night to a two-night stay while checking in at the front desk.

Michael's next stop would be enjoying a nice dinner in the hotel's very own wine bistro called "The Club." Luckily, the maître d' seated him at a table close to the open-air fireplace with a great view of the terrace and garden. He ordered a black Angus steak with baked potato, fresh garden greens, and corn bread. The server recommended a cabernet sauvignon to complement his meal.

He found the food and wine delicious, and his stay was feeling like a short vacation. A country and western band played in the background. The entire scene reminded Michael of Montana. He would have paid more for such a marvelous meal in California, and he was quite sure that the atmosphere wouldn't have been any more sophisticated than this place. He was glad that he had changed into a fresh shirt before going to the bistro as the people around him were elegantly dressed.

After ending his dinner and enjoying an additional glass of wine, he listened to the band for a little longer before going back to his room. The diary of a Colt weaponsmith waited there for him.

He relaxed under a long, hot shower in the spacious bathroom of his suite and admired the slate tiles while standing below the big shower head. Wherever he traveled, Michael collected interior design ideas to use when he built his dream home on an acre of land next to his parents' ranch—someday soon.

As he walked back into the bedroom, he was thrilled to see a coffee maker standing on the small table next to the TV set. He prepared the prepackaged grounds to make coffee and sat in the rocking chair close by.

When his coffee finished brewing, Michael put the full cup on the small table, grabbed the diary and started to read. In the first few pages, Ludwig described how much his family had disappointed and betrayed him. He wrote about his fear of having to live the life of a homeless beggar.

> If not for my job in Mr. Colt's company, I would have been lost. I furnished a small chamber close to the production hall where I can sleep and tend to my work at my desk during the day. It is a small room, but I do not mind. I would rather hide in there than to be among people. I don't sleep well and prefer to work when it is dark as nightmares about their betrayal bother me in my sleep.
>
> I am proud that Samuel Colt selected me to construct the army's new six-shooter. But it saddens me that I cannot share my success with anyone. I still don't understand what got into my father that he treats me so terribly. Am I not his son as well? Is my brother Leopold worth so much more? I admit he works for my father's company, but I'm successful, as well. If I'm able to build the gun the way

> I plan it, the Colt 45 will be a weapon
> that will help write American history and
> decide many battles in the West.

Michael could comprehend the disappointment that the young man felt. He was an only child and had always had a great relationship with his parents. But he knew of many families where siblings fought against each other like cats and dogs. Quite often it was the interference of the parents that resulted in their children turning into rivals.

He refilled his coffee mug and returned to the comfortable rocking chair. Through chapter after chapter, it became clear that Ludwig's hurt feelings turned into anger and hate. Especially at one point it was more than obvious that the relationship between him and his family had been destroyed for good.

> I tried to talk to my father again today. I
> don't want to lose my family and I miss
> my mother very dearly. I feel abandoned
> without her. When I arrived at the house,
> my father didn't bother to listen to me. He
> turned his back on me and went straight
> into his study as if I were a stranger.
>
> I still don't understand how things
> could get to the point where they are now.
> I can only guess that my brother Leopold
> is responsible for the coldness displayed
> toward me.
>
> When I tried to defend my position and
> emphasize that I'm a son of the family with
> a right to be in the house, too, father called
> for Leopold. That freeloader grabbed me

by the collar and beat me. He threw me out of the house as if I were a burglar. My own brother broke my nose. The neighbors stood around watching the scene as if it were a play in a theater.

Never in my entire life have I been so embarrassed and felt so humiliated, and I hate them both from the bottom of my heart for doing this to me. I will never be able to return home. The shame I'm feeling is boundless.

Not only have I lost my family but also my birthright. I really wish I could pay them back. They don't deserve to live a happy life and be rich while they cheated me and took away what belongs to me. They destroyed my once-happy home and stole my life.

This is not a family. These are criminals and I really wish they were dead. If only I knew a way to destroy them the same way.

Although Michael understood the way Ludwig must have felt, nevertheless, he was deeply shocked. The young man had sincerely wished for his own relatives to die.

There weren't many pages left to read. He was a bit disappointed that so far, the diary hadn't given him any clues about the whereabouts of the gun he sought. Was his trip to Fredericksburg in vain?

Oh, come on, Hoss, nothing is in vain. After all, you have a two-day vacation at this wonderful resort. You enjoyed a fantastic meal and will most likely sleep well in this luxury accommodation. Plus, don't forget the excellent country band you heard. This is almost like a weekend back home in Montana.

Michael returned his attention to the diary. It was already past 9:00 p.m., and he didn't expect to encounter any more important information. Nevertheless, he decided to read the entire diary. Reading the whole thing would show respect for the dead weaponsmith named Schmied.

> Today I met a strange man in town. He asked for directions to the Colt factory building. Since I had finished my errands and was about to head back to the company, I offered to take him along.
>
> He wanted to know what my function was at Mr. Colt's factory. I told him that I am responsible for the construction of a new six-shooter. He remarked that my family must be very proud of me since Mr. Colt has entrusted me with such an important task.
>
> I don't know if he noticed my bitterness because he said something rather strange to me: "Sometimes a family doesn't deserve a good son, but maybe other people appreciate the same man much more. Those who destroy our hearts don't really deserve to be part of our lives or to exist at all."
>
> What an odd thing to say. It almost seemed as if he knew my story, but I had never seen the man before. I watched him closely with a sidelong glance and noticed that his eyes were quite dark, almost black. I have never seen a person which such

unnaturally large irises. His hair was also black, and his facial features appeared exotic. Nonetheless, he spoke without any accent.

"Ludwig, you have everything you need to create a tool that could help you to get rid of your father and brother. It's in your own hands to take revenge for the injustice that you faced. I can help you with it."

I was astonished that the stranger knew my first name. Has the rumor about me being thrown out of my family in the most embarrassing way become the talk of the town? Uncontrollable anger seared through me as I considered the possibility. I asked the stranger what he meant when he said that he could help me. He gazed at me for a long moment, his piercing eyes making me uncomfortable.

He mentioned that I could kill two birds with one stone. I didn't know what he meant or what this odd fellow wanted from me. I felt uneasy in his company, but he seemed to understand how I felt.

"Go back to your work, Ludwig. I don't doubt at all that you will create a wonderful and amazing gun. I'm sure the army will be very satisfied with the new weapon. I drew up a few construction ideas which you will find in this letter."

"Originally, I planned to meet Mr. Samuel Colt, but I can save time since the very man who will construct the army revolver stands before me. I wish you all the best,

Ludwig Schmied. I'm convinced that you will write history with this model of the Colt 45, a true gun of destiny."

How in the world did he know about this order? I must have looked dumbfounded, staring at that letter in my hand, not knowing what to do next. When I turned around to ask him further questions, he was gone.

I looked up and down the street, but he was nowhere to be seen. I guess he had disappeared around the corner of the building. Maybe the countless sleepless nights had taken their toll on me.

I went back inside and headed to my little room where I sat at my desk. It was about time to finish the construction plans for the new six-shooter.

Michael Kent wondered about that dark-haired stranger. How come he knew so much about Ludwig's family trouble and his work? The gunsmith must have been the talk of the town, just like young Schmied assumed. Curious, he continued reading the diary.

After I put away my purchases, I opened the envelope. I wondered why my name was written on the outside. How could that be if the stranger was supposed to meet Mr. Colt? Maybe that letter was meant for me right from the start.

Inside the envelope I found a couple of papers that showed drawings of numerous technical details. One can imagine my surprise when I realized that it was a construction plan of a 45-caliber revolver.

I compared his drawings with the ones that I had already finished. I reeled in disbelief when I realized that his construction plans contained solutions to the problematic details I hadn't yet worked out. I don't know the identity of the strange man, but he was definitely a brilliant gunsmith. His drawings showed that he possessed an outstanding technical talent. I immediately realized that his ideas in combination with my designs would very likely create the most successful weapon that Samuel Colt has produced so far.

Michael hesitated. How was that possible? Had Samuel Colt hired a second gunsmith without telling Ludwig? If that was the case, Michael doubted that another gunsmith would have showed the results of his work to a competitor. And why in the world was Ludwig's name written on the envelope? The stranger never could have known that he would meet Ludwig that particular day. After all, he was supposed to meet Samuel Colt.

"Damn it, this doesn't make sense," Michael mumbled. On the next diary page, his notes clearly showed how excited Ludwig Schmied had become about his progress as he constructed the new gun.

It seemed as if the young gunsmith developed an obsession for the revolver. His handwriting became more and more erratic, and his choice of words was increasingly aggressive. Hateful remarks against his father and brother occurred on almost every page now.

Finally, Michael reached the end of the diary where the last few lines were hardly legible. Ludwig's handwriting had changed completely. After trying to decode the scribbling unsuccessfully a couple of times, Michael was finally able to read the last words written by Ludwig Schmied.

I went to the market today. Imagine my surprise when I ran into that stranger again. He asked me about my progress in constructing the six-shooter. I told him how happy I was to meet him as I want to thank him for giving me his excellent suggestions. I asked him how in the world he had figured out the perfect parts to use, even though he had not been included in the design process.

At first, he didn't answer, and I wondered if he was the kind of man who did not like to share his secrets. I waited patiently but have to admit I could not look him straight in the eye. Those eyes are so dark they resemble pieces of coal. It seems as if he can look right to the bottom of your soul. He gives off an eerie feeling, and I become uncomfortable in his presence.

After a long pause, he told me that he possesses a significant knowledge of weapons from all over this world. I asked him how I could thank him, but admitted, shamefully, that I hardly had enough money to buy my own meals. But he just smiled and confused me with the following words: "My dear Ludwig, you could never offer me anything material which would make me richer than I already am. Money is something that I will always possess, and I will never run short of it. Do you remember when I told you that I can hand you a tool to obtain revenge for the injustice that you have faced? Do you remember when I told you that you can right the wrong that was done against you?"

Of course, I remembered those words. I nodded but remained silent. I didn't know what he meant, and I did not want to think about the betrayal that had happened to me. It hurt me too deeply and I will never forgive my family. The hate has grown in me like a hurtful, dangerous ulcer. "May God forgive me, but I even wished for my father's and brother's death. They didn't think twice about whether I ended up in a gutter. They didn't care that I might starve or never see my beloved mother again. They played a cruel game with me, and they do not deserve to live the rest of their lives happily."

"Well, my dear friend, I assume that the firearm is finished by now?"

Again, the stranger seemed know more than what I had told him.

He pressed me. "Have you tested the Colt yet?"

I confirmed that I had, and explained we have a small shooting range behind the production building. But that weird fellow just shook his head.

"No, my dear Ludwig. I'm not talking

about merely testing the functions of the weapon. Shouldn't you make sure that this Colt 45 has the kind of deadly aim that decides life and death for its future owner? I advise you to test it on a living target. I can assure you that this revolver will bring justice upon traitors."

At first, I didn't understand what he meant. Was he suggesting that I should test this firearm by shooting someone?

He abruptly pointed across the market square.

"Look over there, Ludwig, and you will see the perfect targets to prove what an amazingly talented gunsmith you are. Imagine, you can teach the people who have done you so wrong a lesson at the same time."

I looked in the direction he pointed and was shocked to see my father and my brother Leopold in a lively discussion with one of the traders. I couldn't believe my eyes. Was he really suggesting that I should shoot my own father and brother?

Just as I was about to ask him if he was out of his mind, he put his hand on my shoulder and whispered, "Look at those two men, Ludwig. It seems they have a lot of fun together, and they don't waste a single thought on you. Wouldn't it be fair for you to be at your father's side as well? Aren't you his son, too, and don't you deserve to walk by his side? What sin have you committed to be treated like this? They took your home and life away from you, and your brother

> stole your inheritance. You are ostracized
> and treated like an outcast. You're not even
> allowed to see your own mother, Ludwig."

Michael dropped the diary in his lap and stared out the window of the hotel room, aghast. Although he read the diary more than one hundred years after it was written, he was mortified that the stranger would suggest such a thing. So, this was the reason Ludwig Schmied had done away with his family members. He followed the advice of a man he'd never met. Michael read on to see how the story played out.

> The man with the dark eyes continued.
> "No, my dear friend, you didn't do any-
> thing wrong. You're a victim of your
> brother's greed. You struggle in poverty
> while the two of them live like noblemen,
> enjoying their wealth. Haven't you created
> an important weapon that will most likely
> decide the destiny of many men in battle?
> Aren't you the better son?
>
> "Your work for Samuel Colt will be
> known for many years to come. You are
> worth much more than the two of them put
> together. If you ask me, they don't deserve
> to live. Wouldn't it be the biggest satisfac-
> tion of all if you could take revenge with
> the very tool that you yourself created?"
>
> I answered this tempting voice. "Of
> course, I have thought about taking revenge
> while I lie awake all those painful nights
> since I left my father's house. I couldn't

come up with how to bring justice on them." The longer I thought about it the more I realized that this stranger was right. Wouldn't it be ironic if my father and my dishonest brother feared me?

I admit that I began to like the idea. After all, I had nothing to lose. They'd taken everything away from me, and I was not foolish enough to believe that I would ever achieve the same kind of living standard that I had been used to in childhood.

"Think about it, Ludwig, you hold in your own hands the means to follow the path of vendetta. I guarantee you, that six-shooter will never fail if it is used according to its purpose. It is a Colt 45 of destiny and much more than an ordinary firearm. This weapon means justice for you, Ludwig. It's about time for you to get even with them."

I glanced over to my father and brother and observed how they strolled across the market square, in their best moods. It hurt, but at the same time I felt an uncontrollable hate rushing through me like a burning flame. The man was right.

When I turned to tell him so, he was gone. I tried to find him among the crowd but without any luck. Again, I had failed to find out more about him.

Michael sat in his rocking chair and stared at the diary in his lap. He felt overwhelmed with horror. Who was this stranger who knew such personal details about Ludwig, and who advised Ludwig to commit the worst crime in God's eyes?

At first Michael assumed that the dark-haired man was just another gunsmith hired by Samuel Colt. But according to Ludwig's diary it seemed as if he had searched out Ludwig in particular and had not been in touch with the owner of the firearms company at all.

"How in the world could he have suggested that the young lad kill his own father and brother?"

Michael got up and walked over to the minibar where he selected a small bottle of whiskey. He seldom drank hard liquor, but after reading Ludwig's story he needed a sip of the corn juice to calm his nerves.

Since Michael knew that the young gunsmith had followed the stranger's advice and shot his own family members, the diary was even more unnerving to read.

"Sweet Jesus, that young fellow's notes are as dramatic as the ones of Padre de la Vega," he mumbled into the empty room while taking a sip of the golden liquid from the glass in his hand. He felt the cowboy elixir warming the inside of his throat and stomach.

Michael always had a particular liking for the classic guns made by the Colt Firearms Company. The eerie stranger mentioned in Ludwig's diary was right about one thing: the seven-and-a-half-inch SAA Colt 45 had indeed written history, just as the stranger had predicted. It had become the gun that won the West. It saddened Michael that the constructor of such an amazing firearm died under tragic circumstances.

It was around 10:30 p.m., but Michael wanted to finish reading the diary, as he promised Frieda, he would return it during their lunch the next day. There were only about one and a half pages left, so he took another sip of whiskey and picked up the little book.

I am alone. Mrs. Colt put the tray with my dinner in front of the door to my little chamber but I'm not hungry. I cannot forget the image of my laughing father and the way he and Leopold strolled cheerfully through the market square.

All these years I have admired my father and wanted to be just like him. He was my role model and so was my brother Leopold. But they are not the kind of people one should look up to. Rather the opposite is the case. They are both cold-hearted and cruel. They treated me like a beggar or a stray dog that gets kicked down the porch stairs.

My Colt rests in front of me on the table. Yes, it is my weapon. After all, I created it although I have to admit that I had some help with the tricky technical details.

The stranger must be a genius as a gun-smith. It's a shame I never found out his name. I fear him for some reason. I've never met another human being like him. How did he come to know so much about me and my family's situation? How is it possible that he recognized my father and brother today?

I imagine I'm the town laughingstock, and I'm sure everyone thinks I'm a loser who was thrown out of the house overnight. Most likely that man heard my story in one of the drinking holes where the low lives have nothing to do but gossip and drink the entire day.

Dang, he's right. I should really test the

marksmanship of this fine weapon. It fits my hand well and is beautifully crafted. There it is—the serial number. I know it's not the number that Mr. Colt had selected, but I miss my beloved mother so much that I want to dedicate this first model to her by using her birthdate as the serial number.

The cylinder of the revolver turns smoothly, and the Colt is well balanced. But I wonder if I'm developing a problem with my hands lately as every time, I hold this pistol, my palm and fingers turn numb. Luckily, I've never dropped the gun.

The first time this numbness appeared was two weeks ago. If I'm not able to use my hand, I will also lose my job. Then I'd really end up as a beggar on the street, and that scares me more than anything else.

My family is responsible for all my worries and sorrows. I do hate them from the bottom of my heart. It is true—those two men deserve to die. Why should I give up everything I had without fighting for it? Most likely they think I'm a weak toddler who can be pushed around however it pleases them, but they underestimated my grit.

I will teach them a lesson and let them tremble with fear. I want them to beg for their lives, and I want them to lose everything just like I did. I have the power to destroy their lives like they took away mine. My beautifully crafted Colt 45, you and I will bring justice upon them together.

Shaken, Michael closed the leatherbound diary. To hear the story told by Frieda over a cup of coffee was one thing but to read the personal thoughts of a murderer was a completely different experience. Michael felt he had personally witnessed the tragic events.

He downed the rest of his whiskey. The image of Ludwig and his new weapon bothered him. The young man must have known that by the end of that pivotal night, not only his father and brother would be dead. Michael was sure that he also planned to commit suicide right after the six-shooter had fulfilled its cruel task.

There were six bullets in the gun's cylinder, more than enough to send three men straight to hell.

"He shot a bullet into his brain after killing his own flesh and blood—more or less the same ending as in Johnny Ringo's case," Michael mused while returning the empty glass to the tray next to the coffee maker.

He glanced over at the second diary he had read within a week, recounting such horrible events. Never in his wildest dreams would Michael Kent have expected that the search for a gun would lead him into the midst of so many human tragedies. A double murder in Hartford, Connecticut, and only a few years later the same drama unfolding in Santa Fe, New Mexico, carried out by a young boy.

Michael was on the way to the bathroom but hesitated. "Now wait a minute, both crimes happened within a family. In both cases the son shot his own father or father and brother. Both diaries describe the same kind of drama and background. Could that be a coincidence? And let's not forget Johnny Ringo, who shot himself."

Michael walked around the room thinking aloud. "What did Padre de la Vega write? Young Josef found the weapon somewhere in a cave in the mountains. Why had the boy insisted that the man of the Bible should bring the Colt 45 to a safe Christian place and keep it hidden there?"

He stopped to gaze out the window and continued aloud with his speculation. "One would think that so shortly before his execution, everything else would be of a higher priority to him, like confessing his sins or begging for forgiveness. Why was it more urgent for the boy to instruct the padre to take care of the gun rather than saving his own soul? That doesn't make sense. Josef murdered his own father. The Padre's diary gives the impression that Josef saw the revolver as a personal enemy, and even more so, that he feared the weapon."

Michael paced up and down inside the comfortable log cabin. An incredible thought intruded into his mind. "What if it was the same weapon in both of those cases? It can't be coincidence that the two stories are so alike. When I compare the two diaries it seems that history has repeated itself."

The expert on historical firearms concluded there was only one way to find out if it really had been the same weapon implicated in both family dramas.

Michael knew that de la Vega had Johnny Ringo's Colt. The serial number had been registered during the trial against Josef Hernandez, and the Benedictine monk wrote it down in his diary. It would be outrageous if that specific revolver was the first model of its kind constructed by no one lesser then Ludwig Schmied.

It would raise the worth of the Colt 45 immensely. Michael wondered if Conway assumed that he was looking for a priceless gun. It would explain the collector's passion and determination.

Michael opened the sliding door to the small private terrace outside his room. He looked over at the softly lit restaurant and enjoyed the cool evening air. The beautifully kept garden and the fresh air help him sort through his thoughts.

"How can I find a connection between the two cases?" he asked the cool night air. He studied the lush flower beds and the cleverly arranged spotlights between the trees and the flowering bushes.

Not far from his cabin he heard the gurgling sound of a fountain that rose from the center of a placid pond. Water lilies added to the romantic atmosphere. Michael thought about his mother. She would have loved this place.

"Mother … That's it. Why haven't I thought of this earlier? The serial number of Ludwig Schmied's prototype gun is the same as his mother's birthday. That's what he wrote. If I can find out what day her birthday was, I will have proof that the same Colt 45 was the perpetrator in these two dramas."

***

Michael decided to hit the sack. It had been a long and strenuous day and he was tired. But the exertions were well worth it, as he had found an important clue in Ludwig's notes despite his earlier doubts.

Although his bed was comfortable, he didn't sleep soundly. Nightmares about the man with piercing, dark eyes haunted his repose. The following day he drove to Frieda's house and picked up the elder lady for his lunch date.

When she opened the front door, he handed her the book with the notes by her relative and thanked her for the trust she had shown by lending it for an entire evening. She carefully put the book back into the wooden treasure box. Then she grabbed her purse and a light jacket and took the arm of the good-looking young men who escorted her to the passenger side of his car. He opened the door for her like the true gentleman he was.

Frieda directed him to a typical German restaurant which was famous for its traditional cuisine. After their host had guided them to a table in the Old German Bakery, they ordered their food.

Frieda decided on a classical Wiener schnitzel with potato salad and Michael couldn't resist the sauerbraten, a rump roast marinated in red wine.

After their friendly server brought their beverages, Frieda came straight to the point. "Has Ludwig's diary helped you to find out what you need to know Michael?"

"I think so. It's not easy to read, especially the last few pages. They are quite shocking, aren't they? Considering that you are a family member it must have saddened you deeply to go through those pages."

Frieda held her glass with both hands and looked at him over the rim. "I had always heard only one side of the story. The entire family never had a good opinion of Ludwig. To all my relatives, it was clear that he was nothing but a coward and murderer.

After reading his diary I was able to understand his despair, at least to a certain degree. The injustice he faced doesn't provide grounds for murder, but I do believe that a human being with a broken heart is not able to act and behave as rationally. After all, the people closest to him betrayed him horribly.

The thing that still bugs me are the chapters he wrote about that odd stranger, who seemed to know so much about Ludwig and the family crisis. I somehow have the feeling that this man had influenced Ludwig in an evil way, and my guess is that he is partly responsible for that terrible shooting. I can't stop wondering who that man was."

Michael nodded. "Yes, I wondered about that too. It

seems as if that mysterious stranger met Ludwig on purpose for the sake of talking him into that terrible crime. By the way, had anybody ever mentioned what happened to the murder weapon after your relative had committed suicide?"

"No, but there are rumors that Samuel Colt paid for the pauper's grave behind the cemetery's wall. I would imagine that the owner of the firearms company brought the weapon back to the production building. After all it was the prototype for a huge army order which he had to deliver. Without the prototype revolver he couldn't have started production, could he?"

"You are one smart woman, Frieda. I should have thought of that myself. Of course, Mr. Colt must have taken the six-shooter back to his factory. Ludwig was the one who constructed it and tragically tested it, but it still belonged to the owner of the firearms company."

The server returned to their table and placed their mouthwatering meals before them. Michael's sauerbraten was delicious, and Frieda seemed equally happy with her chosen schnitzel.

"Frieda, you know what? I really like Fredericksburg. I'll like to visit you again this fall when they harvest the grapes."

"You will always be warmly welcomed, dear friend. Bring your mother along. She would feel at home here considering her German roots."

Michael laughed. "Oh yeah, I already see myself carrying tons of German cookbooks and souvenirs which my poor father would have to find extra space for at home on the ranch in Montana." Frieda's hearty laughter made him smile.

After finishing their food, they continued their conversation. "Frieda, I do have one question. It might sound a bit weird, but do you know the date of birth of your great-grandaunt, Ludwig's mom?"

"You want to find out what serial number he engraved on that Colt, right?"

Again, Michael was astonished at the sharp mind the elderly lady possessed. He nodded.

"Well, Michael, you are lucky. Ludwig's mother was three years older than my great-grandfather. Since they were siblings, he painted a so-called family tree. He was really talented, you know."

"Oh, but I'm wandering off the point. I saw the date Ludwig's mom was born painted on the picture. It was during a severe February. She almost died as a baby. It was bitterly cold, and the family was far too poor to be able to afford a better oven and firewood at that time. Her birthday was on February 22nd. She was born under the zodiac sign of Pisces."

Michael blanched and his heart skipped a beat. He set his glass aside. There it was, the serial number 222 of the very Colt caliber 45 that he was looking for and which was known as Johnny Ringo's six-shooter.

Michael Kent didn't search for any lesser weapon than the famous prototype of the pistol that wrote American history and had killed at least four family members who turned against each other like packs of hungry wolves.

"Are you okay, Michael?" Frieda asked with a worried look.

"Yes, I just remembered something that I discovered during my research and have to verify it. It looks like Ludwig's Colt 45 has caused further misery over the years. I can't tell you more than that, but I promise to keep you up to date as soon as I know more."

Frieda brought her hand to her mouth. "Oh, my God, you mean this weapon has been used in the same fatal way in other families? I was sure that Samuel Colt kept it in a museum or in the archive of the company."

Michael nodded grimly. "Let's put it this way. The serial number showed up years later under similar circumstances. But I don't want to worry you unnecessarily. I need to gather a few facts first to make sure. You understand, don't you? By the way, has anybody ever tried to convince you to sell the diary?"

Up to now Michael hadn't mentioned his client's name. Whether it was a gut feeling or suspicions based on their conversation, he couldn't recall.

"Oh yes, one man tried to buy the diary. One day he suddenly stood at my door and offered me quite a nice amount for the little book. He told me that he was a collector and asked me all sorts of questions about the contents of Ludwig's notes. I told him that I had read them all."

"I openly admit that I disliked the man from the first moment. He was a creepy fellow. He got pretty pushy when he realized I didn't want to sell the diary. He left only after I reassured him that no clues about the whereabouts of the gun were mentioned in the book. That was when I realized that he was not at all interested in Ludwig's story but wanted to know more about the Colt 45."

Frieda shifted in her chair. "I'm sure he was one of those crazy obsessed firearm collectors who fill their entire house with rifles and pistols to show off for their friends."

"If I recall it correctly, he showed up two or three years ago. I'm not sure about the exact date, though. You know, once you get older your memory gets weaker. But I will never forget his face with those eerie, piercing eyes. His name was Conway. Ludwig or the reputation of my family obviously didn't matter to him. I advised him to get in touch with the Colt Firearms Company and convinced him that most likely the gun had been returned to them after my poor ancestor's death."

Michael remained silent. He understood Frieda's distrust of Conway well. He even shared it to a certain degree and couldn't deny the man was strange. Indeed, Conway had lied to him in "forgetting" to mention that he had tried to buy the diary from Frieda. Indeed, when Michael brought up the trip to Fredericksburg, Conway had pretended that he thought the diary had no value to their quest.

Michael wasn't obligated in that he had returned Ludwig's notes to her. He found the important clue that he was hoping for, and he wanted to avoid damaging the reputation of the young gunsmith any further.

Michael was certain that the family had suffered more than enough due from the tragic circumstances. When he read the newspaper clipping about Ludwig Schmied, he had wondered why the diary was not among Conway's possessions already. Now he understood that Ludwig's story was not important enough for Conway. The man wasn't interested in the people behind the story, a fact that didn't make the collector more likable.

When the server returned to the table with the check, Michael was happy that he had a chance to reciprocate for Frieda's generosity and help and quickly grabbed the bill. He really liked the lady and would do his best to find out the truth. He knew it was a matter of honor for her family.

The firearms expert drove Frieda Miller home where they bid farewell. Michael planned to make use of the remains of the day by doing further research on his computer and laying out his strategy on how to continue the search for the famous pistol. He was relieved that he had another night to rest before flying back to California.

CHAPTER NINE

***

ARCHIVES OF COLT FIREARMS COMPANY

As soon as he was back at the resort, he set up his laptop and made himself comfortable on the well-furnished terrace of his cabin. He enjoyed a cup of the coffee he had brewed in his room and wrote an email to his cousin, the brother in the monastery of the Benedictine Order in Switzerland.

In the letter, he mentioned he was in the middle of some research about a Padre de la Vega and asked his cousin Alexander if there was any possibility of getting access to the archives of their monastery in Switzerland. He explained that he hoped to find out more about de la Vega, who had been a monk of the same order and most likely appeared somewhere among the registry of Benedictine members. He asked him to call him or to answer to his email as soon as possible and thanked him in advance.

Michael knew that it wasn't easy to get access to any of the archives of the Roman Catholic Church. Therefore, he didn't mention the search for the gun but kept some of the facts to himself until he could meet Alexander face-to-face.

Next on his to-do list was a long-overdue call to his friend Peter O'Riley. Peter had an important position in the Colt Firearms Company. Peter owed him a favor as Michael had helped his friend purchase an original Winchester rifle formerly owned by actor John Wayne in an auction.

Luckily, he picked up the phone right away.

"Hello, Peter. It's me, Michael Kent. How's the gun business?"

"Hey, Michael. Great to hear from you. So far, so good, I'd say. We have lots of orders lately. How are you doing?"

"Can't complain at all. If people continue to seek my expertise the way they do right now, my dream of my own ranch in Montana is closer than ever. I really miss that open, free land and scenery, you know. To be honest, California is starting to feel too crowded and hectic for me. Costs and traffic are equally annoying."

"I can imagine. But hey, I know you well enough to know that you don't call just to say hi. So, what's up, dude? Can I do something for you?"

"Peter, you're right, and I don't want to beat around the bush. This new client who hired me is very interested in a nineteenth century army Colt. To be frank, he is searching for the first revolver of its kind. This collector urgently wants to own the prototype of the seven-and-a-half-inch Single Action Army Colt 45 which was originally constructed by your company for the U.S. army."

Peter whistled through his teeth. "I'll be darned, you're not talking about the weapon constructed by this unlucky chap whose secret chamber we found during demolition work three years ago, do you?"

Michael laughed. "Bingo, my friend. As usual you hit the nail right on the head."

"Michael, you selected quite a hard nut to crack. You

know I've always been interested in historical weapons, and maybe I can help you this time and save you unnecessary research. Some time ago I was interested in the whereabouts of that prototype model myself. I sacrificed a free weekend and hid myself for more than sixteen hours in that dusty old archive in our management building. Since then, we've filed everything electronically, but there are still account books, delivery lists and construction plans that aren't electronically archived.

"To be frank, I'd expected that Mr. Colt or his descendants kept that six-shooter to display it in our little museum. It was one of the biggest and most significant orders put in during the startup years of this company. But the gun isn't in the museum. Apparently old Samuel hasn't kept the six-shooter anywhere near the company at all."

"I found one of the old production lists, which at that time were still handwritten by Samuel Colt himself. He numbered that very revolver number one but wrote down the original serial number that its constructor Schmied had engraved, and which read as 222.

Michael interjected. "I discovered that '222' was the serial number of the prototype."

Peter continued his story. "My friend, you won't believe this. A couple of hours later I stumbled across the same serial number again. It was recorded on a bill of lading to a cavalry troop stationed somewhere in the southwest of the Arizona territory. The Army maintained a couple of forts there. We delivered a larger shipment to the boys during the years of the Apache wars. At first it astonished me that he had allowed the prototype of this fine weapon to be mixed in with common firearms. But then I saw a handwritten note on the bill of lading for that shipment. Apparently, the big boss himself had written it. After reading it I understood why he had let the gun go. He had written down clear orders that this specific firearm should be added to the shipment free of charge so that he and his company would be relieved of that sinister revolver for good."

On the other end of the call, Michael remained silent, but sucked in a sharp breath. The stories of the murders committed by the gun darted through his mind. He had difficulty focusing on what his friend was saying.

"Believe me, Michael, up to today I don't understand why Colt thought so little of the very weapon that saved his firearm company from bankruptcy. But the order is unambiguous, so the Colt 45 was sent West with the large delivery, and no money was collected for it. If I recall correctly, the crates were shipped to Fort Bowie south of Tucson where the soldiers in blue uniforms still faced troubles created by the Apache at that time."

"Wow Peter, you really helped me with this information, and indeed spared me lots of time of doing research. The next complicated case I am after I will call you right away so we can ride the same boat right from the start."

Peter laughed loud. "Do you really think that the few facts I told you can help you find that revolver? That peace-maker can literally be anywhere or most likely it no longer exists and lies in pieces in the Sonora Desert between a bunch of thorny cacti."

"Dang sure it helps me. I found a clue that suggests it changed ownership from a soldier in the army to no one lesser than a famous outlaw of the Old West who had been using that Peacemaker for quite some time. I can't spill the beans yet, but I promise I'll keep you up to date about the story."

"Holy cow, that sounds exciting. I'm really looking for-ward to hearing more about it. Oh, before I forget, I applied for a few off days this coming summer, and I'm planning to spend a week or so in Montana. It would be great if we could spend a day or two together fly fishing. What do you say?"

"Now if that isn't a lucky coincidence. I'm planning to visit my parents and check out a few properties close to their house since I want to start building my ranch at the latest next year. I'm self-employed, and I can adjust my off days according to your vacation. Let's stay in touch and start planning by late June. But I don't want to bother you and keep you from work any longer. You really helped me, Peter. Thank you so much for the information. I'll send you an email as soon as I know anything new."

Michael could hear the smile in his friend's voice. "You're always welcome. After all, you helped me lay hands on my dream Winchester. She received a place of honor right over the new fireplace in our living room. Okay, hope to hear from you soon, Michael, and good luck with your chase after that Peacemaker."

"Alrighty, talk to you later, Peter. I'm looking forward to our fishing adventure. Take care and be careful with those guns, my friend."

He hung up and gazed outside the log cabin, so lost in thought he didn't see the flower beds. "I'll be darned. The Peacemaker found its way to Arizona. So most likely, Johnny Ringo bought the gun from a soldier or possibly even stole it," he mumbled into the empty room.

Although it seemed impossible at the beginning of his search, Michael had found the trail of the famous pistol, like following its footprints across the country.

Since he couldn't do anything else from Texas, he decided to end the evening with a decent meal and a glass of the excellent Texas wine served at the resort. His flight back to California was scheduled for the next morning.

CHAPTER TEN

***

OVERSEAS FLIGHT INTO THE OLD WORLD

The next morning Michael drank a coffee in the airport terminal and checked his emails. To his surprise, brother Alexander in the Swiss monastery had already answered his inquiry. He assured Michael that Friar Hieronymus who was responsible for the abbey's library had agreed to help him with his search for information about Padre de la Vega.

Many of the old clerical books were written in Latin, and Michael was relieved to have a translator by his side. He thanked his cousin for the trust and offered help. He assured his relative that he would get back to him as soon as he knew his flight dates. His cousin had organized a guest room in the wing of the monastery which was reserved for visitors.

After arriving back in his apartment in Los Angeles that evening, he called his client Mr. Conway. However, he didn't want to reveal to the man all the details of his research in Texas.

Conway picked up the phone on the first ring. He sound-ed gruff, but when he heard Michael's voice, he tried his best to muster a friendlier tone.

"Mr. Kent, how is the investigation going?" As usual, the man got straight to the point. But this time Michael was prepared for it and remained self-confident. The impatience of others was nothing new to him, as many collectors were just like Mr. Conway.

"Not bad at all, but I agree with you that the search needs to follow Father de la Vega, just as you assumed before. I will need to find out to which Benedictine monastery the good padre moved to after leaving Santa Fe. You see, the Benedictine order is famous for recording their history in chronicles. Therefore, I am in high hopes that I will be able to find out if Padre de la Vega returned to Spain, and if so, where. Chances are, there might be even a clue about whether he still carried the gun with him or what he did with it. Unfortunately, to do so it will create additional costs, as I would have to fly to Europe. So, I would really understand if you'd..."

But Conway interrupted him immediately. "Book your flight and whatever you need. I will transfer $5000 to your account immediately after this call for the ticket, a hotel and meal expenses. Fly to Europe as quickly as possible and keep me informed, Mr. Kent. I don't care about the time difference since I'm a night person anyway."

There it was again, the commanding tone which Michael had disliked right from the start. But he had to admit, that the man was generous beyond expectations. He hadn't hesitated at all to cover the travel expenses and even more.

Michael wondered how obsessed his client was with this gun. It almost seemed like some sort of holy relic to him. Because of his consuming, treasure-hunting behavior, Michael told Conway only that he found proof that Johnny Ringo's revolver had indeed been one of the first of that production series, but he didn't mention it was the prototype. He promised Conway to keep him constantly informed either via email or via phone and then hung up. He couldn't say why, but he found the conversations with Conway distasteful. He thought about Frieda Miller, who felt the same kind of aversion for the man.

But his feelings about the elderly lady in Texas were totally opposite. Meeting her had been a pleasant surprise. "Oh well, try to think positive. After all, you are going to visit your cousin Alexander whom you haven't seen in ages. And you can travel to beautiful Switzerland without paying a cent for it. Now if that ain't a nice treat, then I don't know what is. I already hear my mother dictating a long list of souvenirs from the Old World which I will likely have to bring back home," he mumbled while he checked the online platform for overseas flights. "Don't forget the chocolate and a Swiss watch and how about these funny Edelweiss suspenders for your father..." he imagined her saying.

After checking the flight details, he looked into his bank account and saw that Conway's payment had already been transferred. To his relief Michael found a nonstop Swissair flight from Los Angeles to Zurich International Airport and booked one of the few remaining seats on it two days later.

The following day he packed his luggage and made sure that he had enough clothes for at least ten days. Michael had no idea how long the research in Switzerland would take, or if he would need to continue his travels to the Spanish monastery where de la Vega most likely spent the last years of his life. Fortunately, all Benedictine monasteries were constantly in contact with each other.

When he finally called his parent's home in Montana and informed his mother about the planned trip to Switzerland, she was very excited about it, just as Michael had expected. Of course, she insisted that Michael buy one of those famous Swiss watches for his father and a whole bunch of the decadent Swiss chocolates for her friends.

She was so thrilled about his planned trip that she didn't stop talking, and Michael had to cut her short, explaining that he had to finish packing. His fourteen hour flight left early in the morning from LAX.

He went to bed early but was too excited to sleep. Despite the long flight he was very much looking forward to the trip to beautiful Europe.

When he got up the next morning, he felt tired and drank strong coffee after taking a cold shower. Luckily, his suitcase was already packed, and he had checked in online the previous evening, so he had more than enough time to get to the airport without stress. Less than two hours later he took the exit to Los Angeles International Airport.

The overseas flight lasted eleven hours, and Michael tried his best to kill time by watching movies, reading a book, and sleeping. He knew that it wouldn't be easy to overcome the nine hours' time difference and jet lag from the time zone change.

After landing in Zurich and picking up his suitcase from the luggage carousel he went straight to the underground area of the airport where trains left directly to the surrounding areas and Swiss cities. He searched the timetable for the next available train which would take him to Einsiedeln in about forty minutes.

He was tired and ready to hit the sack although it was only noon, but he enjoyed the scenery racing by the huge windows of the train. He had to admit that traveling on public transportation was comfortable and pleasant in Switzerland. When he arrived at the station of Einsiedeln he immediately found a taxi that took him to the monastery in a little more than ten minutes. Michael didn't know what he expected, but when he saw the facade of the sacred building, he was speechless. The entire monastery complex was indeed impressive.

Alexander had asked him to meet him at the gate that was the side entrance to the church. Thanks to his detailed description, Michael found it immediately. He pulled on the old-fashioned metal doorbell and heard a chime on the other side of the huge wooden door.

It didn't take long before the door opened. In front of Michael stood a smiling Brother Alexander welcoming him with open arms and surprisingly gray hair. He was dressed in the typical black Benedictine monk's cassock.

Alexander hugged his cousin Michael and slapped him cordially on the back. "My God, Michael, I never thought I'd see the day when you come to visit me here within our dignified walls. I'm so happy to see a face from home. How was your flight? Are you hungry? I'm sure you are tired. Do you want to rest first?"

Michael raised his hand placatory. "Hold on for a minute. You are asking way too many questions at once. It is wonderful to see you, Alexander. You're looking great."

Michael didn't exaggerate. Although his hair was gray, Alexander appeared content, and an aura of inner peace surrounded him.

The monk took Michael's suitcase and motioned him to follow while he led the way to the guest rooms. The silence within the long stone hallways was something that Michael had never experienced before. It was not unpleasant but rather the opposite after the hectic buzzing of the airports and the long hours in the crowded plane.

The guest rooms were simply furnished but tidy, and

Michael was relieved to see that a private, small bathroom was attached to the cozy bedroom.

Brother Alexander mentioned the times meals were served and ensured Michael that he as a male guest was of course allowed to eat with the monks of the community. He put the suitcase next to the bed and told his guest that he would like to show him the most important rooms of the monastery first.

"I have to make sure that you find the dining hall where we normally eat our meals."

The two men left the room and followed the same hallway through which they had entered. After showing the dining hall, Alexander walked ahead and followed the old stone staircase which led to the rear of the monastery's side entrance where Michael had rung the doorbell upon his arrival.

Michael's cousin opened another door leading to a large building to the rear of the monastery's gate and motioned Michael to step through it. He hadn't had enough time to study pictures of the monastery's layout as his flight to Switzerland came on such short notice.

When Michael stepped into the church of Einsiedeln Abbey, he wasn't prepared for the splendor awaiting him. The entire building was richly decorated with colorful frescos, statues, and deftly shaped stucco. Countless side chapels were dominated by beautifully worked marble altars holding relics and coffins of the first Christian martyrs. Huge paintings hung above them, and numerous statues created by Europe's most talented sculptors were on display in every cranny of the building. The high ceiling was covered with enormous frescoes showing scenes from the Bible. Numerous sturdy pillars supported the ceiling and separated the nave of the church from the side chapels.

Alexander watched his cousin, who stood marveling at the breathtaking sacred building. "It's beautiful, isn't it?"

Michael shook his head. "I had no idea, Alexander. This is likely the most jaw-dropping church I have ever seen in my entire life. One would expect something like this in Rome, but not here in a small country like Switzerland. I don't even know where to start looking. There is so much art in this building that one doesn't know what to admire first."

Alexander smiled. As always, he was touched by the reaction of people when they first saw the church. To show it to one of his relatives made him proud. He pointed to the rear of the nave. "The church has enough seats for at least 600 worshippers, but back there is the very heart of our monastery." He walked toward a chapel inside the church built completely from black marble. The chapel walls were fifteen feet long and intricately decorated. A life-size statue of an angel stood over the door, twenty feet above their heads.

"As you may know, we venerate Holy Mary in particular. We call this the Chapel of Mercy. Right here was the original location of a little hut originally surrounded by forest where holy Benedict lived until he was killed by two thieves. Numerous miracles were recorded here on this very spot while people prayed to that statue over there above the altar."

He pointed to a black statue inside the chapel embellished with gold and dressed in rich clothes. "As you can see the statue resembles Holy Mary and her son Jesus as an infant. Scientists still argue why the figure is black. It has never been painted. Some say it's because of the smoke of thousands of candles that burned in this chapel over the centuries. Others assume it has to do with the wood that the sculptor selected when he created this statue."

"Well, I have to get back to work. Maybe it would be a good idea for you rest a bit to overcome the time difference. There's a beautiful short hiking trail around the abbey, just in case you want to catch some fresh air after the long flight. You will meet Friar Hieronymus during dinner in the evening. He is the monk who is responsible for our community's entire library. We actually have two libraries in this monastery, and both are equally impressive."

"I think you're right. A bit of fresh air wouldn't hurt. Besides, I might be able to drink a coffee next to the monastery's plaza. I saw some nice coffee shops there. Dinner is in that huge dining hall you showed me at 6 p.m. sharp, right?"

Alexander nodded, waved, and walked back to his small office next to the church gate. By now Michael knew that Alexander handled pilgrim groups as well as people who contacted the Benedictine order for help, special prayers, events and much more.

Michael left the impressive church nave through its main portal and stepped on to the cobblestone plaza. The sun shone overhead, and the temperature felt mild.

Spring flowers blossomed everywhere, and their fragrance filled the air. Some of the cafés had placed tables and chairs outside where people sat to enjoy the sun, drink their coffee, and marvel at the grand view of the façade of the huge sacred building. The two belltowers were in clear view from this angle.

The young American walked toward the nearest coffee shop and sat down at a small bistro table covered with a red checkered cloth. He ordered a cappuccino and one of the famous Swiss chocolate croissants. As he waited for the snack, he studied the impressive façade with its tall towers on either side.

"I should travel more," he mumbled while he looked around. "How beautiful some countries are." When the waitress returned with his cappuccino and the delicious-looking croissant, he quickly snapped a picture of the goodies on his table with the monastery and its cobblestone plaza in the background.

He texted both shots to his mum including the short message **Arrived safely and am enjoying life. Warmest greetings from Switzerland. Your son, Michael.**

It was around 4:30 in the afternoon when Michael stepped into the nave again. He stopped dead in his tracks astonished when he saw that most of the monks stood close together in front of the Chapel of Mercy, praying. Michael recalled that brother Alexander had told him about this short afternoon mass.

Since Michael had been raised according to the Roman Catholic Church, he respectfully stepped between two of the wooden benches a couple of rows behind the monks and listened to their prayer. Thanks to his German mother, he understood quite a few of the German texts.

At the end of the mass the monks chanted a polyphonic Latin hymn dedicated to Holy Mary. It was a mystical Gregorian chorale named *Salve Regina*.

Deeply moved, Michael listened to the chant of the Benedictine monks. He saw his cousin in the front row. Very much to his own surprise, Michael completely forgot about the crazy world outside the church walls. California with all its frantic people seemed to be more distant than ever. This place was definitely a thought-provoking destination.

Michael didn't know if the exhaustion of the long overseas flight or the meditative atmosphere was responsible for making him forgot about his job or his life in Los Angeles.

He couldn't recall when he last felt such an inner peace. Although Michael had attended church regularly when he lived in Montana, he had never been so impressed or captivated by any event in a church before.

When the last tone of the *Salve Regina* chorale faded away, the monks respectfully bent their heads toward the statue of Holy Mary. Then they slowly walked in two orderly lines toward the main alter where they turned to their right and vanished through a small side door.

Michael followed them and pulled the smithed handle of the gate bell once again. The door opened automatically thanks to the tiny button pressed by his cousin in the room next door. He already awaited Michael, but he was not alone. An elder monk with black hair standing next to Alexander greeted him cordially. He bent his head slightly and introduced himself as Friar Hieronymus.

CHAPTER ELEVEN

***

THE ARCHIVES OF THE BENEDICTINE ORDER

"It is a great pleasure to meet a relative of our brother Alexander. He told me that you need my help and plan to do some research in our library. You are more than welcome to start studies tomorrow after our morning prayers and breakfast. Since we still have some time until dinner is served, I would like to show you our wonderful library. We had to extend our archives and many historical books are now stored in one of the most modern libraries in Switzerland."

Michael smiled. "I can't wait to see the Abbey's libraries, Friar Hieronymus."

The Friar nodded. "I do prefer the historical one because of its beauty, but the new one, built only a couple of years ago, offers modern computers and copy machines, and has thermostatically controlled air conditioning to ensure that none of the books suffer damage from moisture or temperature changes. Our collection of books and historical documents is so extensive as to be unbelievable. Sometimes academic collectors pass their holdings on to us when they die. So, the number of books is constantly growing. We hold treasures in those two libraries that will leave you speechless, Mr. Kent," he added with a boyish smile.

"Please, call me Michael," the young American offered.

"Ah, a namesake of Archangel Michael." Alexander's cousin laughed.

"You got that right. That was exactly the reason why my mother named me Michael. She has always honored that particular angel. From my childhood onward she has always been sure that I have a special purpose for God in this world. But I do believe that my cousin here fulfills those expectations much better than I do."

Alexander stared at him. "You never know, Michael. Sometimes the call of God enters our life rather late."

Friar Hieronymus led his guest through countless hallways. After a few minutes Michael wondered if he would be able to remember the way to the dining room the next morning. It was easy to get lost in the huge complex.

"How long have you been living here in this monastery, Friar Hieronymus?"

"Well, I studied theology and then went to Rome for a few years. You could call it the headquarters," he added, laughing softly. "I consider myself lucky because I was allowed to work in the Vatican archives."

Michael stopped dead in his tracks and stared at the Benedictine friar. "Wow, I envy you for that opportunity, Father Hieronymus. I am sure that the collected wisdom in the archives of the Vatican must leave an impression on a man for the rest of his life, doesn't it?"

"Oh yes, I have to agree with that. And some of the things written in those books also change a man for the rest of his life. Believe me Michael, it isn't just a banal saying of our mother church when we preach that evil is among us, walking through this world, influencing it in the worst way. There are countless stories, legends and events that took place, allowing the Holy Church to collect proof for the existence of Satan."

When Michael remained silent, the friar stopped in the middle of the hallway and looked through one of the arched windows into the small park that lay nestled behind the abbey's walls. "Michael, I'm not one of the clergy members who believes that our church is an infallible institution. I am aware of the crimes committed by the Catholic Church over the centuries, and I know that our ecclesial dignitaries often haven't worn a spotless vest as they want people to believe. But trust me, there are writings that would make your hair stand on end, and which test your faith and judgment in the most frightening ways. In other tomes, you will find proof to deepen and strengthen your faith in God and the Catholic Church."

Michael was surprised by the self-criticism, and he immediately understood that Friar Hieronymus was a highly educated human being. *I can consider myself lucky that this outstanding man gives me an opportunity to spend time in the library here. He is helping me with my research and allowing me to enter his world of elevated spirituality.*

Friar Hieronymus stopped in front of an artfully carved double door. Actually, it was more a portal. The monk pulled a big keychain from his black belt which was partly hidden under his robe. He selected a beautifully ornamented key and pushed it carefully into the impressive iron lock under the door handle. The lock sprang open with a loud clicking noise. Friar Hieronymus pushed down on the handle and opened the right panel of the door.

Both men entered an impressive hall which was over a hundred feet long. The ceiling was a marvelous example of baroque art, covered with amazingly detailed murals, stucco medallions and ornaments. The ceiling was arched and stood at least thirty feet above the floor. The walls were covered with bookshelves framed by delicate stucco medallions and marble pillars.

An open gallery led to the second level where each wall was covered with bookshelves. Thousands of books waited for their readers. Many were leather bound and looked extremely old.

Michael couldn't believe his eyes as he stood speechless in the middle of the library. He felt like a child seeing his first Christmas tree. He was certainly glad that he had planned to stay a few days.

"Oh, my God, this is simply fantastic," he exclaimed, but immediately lowered his voice, hushed by the echo inside the hall. He strode along the walls, his face displaying the awe he felt. He admired the beautiful maple floor which flowed together perfectly.

"Our collection spans one thousand years," Friar Hieronymus declared proudly. He pointed to an elegant showcase in the middle of the floor. "This, as an example, is a handwritten Bible that was translated from Hebrew into Latin in the year 1040."

The American was deeply impressed and thanked the monk for granting him the honor of looking at such treasures.

Friar Hieronymus moved his hand in a wide gesture encompassing the library's holdings. "I have studied countless books during the past few decades. It will help me a lot if you tell me what you are looking for tomorrow. That would make things easier for us. At least I would know where I should start the search."

Friar Hieronymus folded his hands in front of him. "Now let me quickly show you our basement archive and then we should head back to the dining hall. My stomach growls worse than a hungry wolf and I'm afraid that the cook might hear it." He laughed loudly about his own joke, and Michael joined him. He liked this humble man's humor right away.

Dinner among monks was the opposite of what Michael had expected. After saying a short prayer, they all ate a simple but delicious meal. Roasted chicken was placed on their plates as the main course with potatoes and seasoned green beans served as accompaniments. The kitchen didn't forget the fresh-baked bread and a delicious pudding for dessert. Once finished most of them stood in small groups absorbed in lively conversations about the day, the news, or other events that took place in the area. One thing they all had in common—they all seemed content and happy.

After a while, the monks wished Michael a good night's rest and walked toward the church for their final prayer of the day, known as the compline. Michael however, walked back to his guest room since the long flight and time difference finally took their toll on him. He was dead tired.

He knew that the Benedictine monks got up very early in each morning to follow their main rule of *ora et labora*, prayer and work. He didn't want to leave a bad impression or annoy Friar Hieronymus. They had agreed on meeting at 8:30 the following day right after breakfast. Michael set his alarm on his smart phone since he didn't trust himself to wake up on time due to jet lag.

Michael slept soundly and dreamlessly, but he woke up early around 4:30 a.m. He groaned when he arose. His spine wasn't used to the small bed with its hard mattress. He was sure that it would take a while until he adapted to the time difference as well.

The bells of the two church towers welcomed the new day at 5:00 a.m. Alexander told Michael that they started the day with prayers before breakfast. He wondered if he could ever get used to that kind of rigorous discipline.

He met Alexander and Friar Hieronymus for breakfast at 7:00 o'clock sharp and was surprised to see how eager to get back to work some of the elders seemed to be. His cousin greeted him warmly.

The expert on guns looked forward to a slice of freshly baked bread and a big piece of the homemade Swiss cheese laid out in the middle of the table. In case the coffee was too weak for his taste he would order a stronger one later in the same coffee shop where he stopped by the previous day.

"Hey Michael, did you sleep well within our sacred walls?"

Michael nodded. "Alexander, after observing the monks of your community I came to the conclusion, that most people beyond these monastery walls should make you their role models when it comes to contentment and diligence."

"Believe me, it's not always easy to live here. We sacrifice a lot. But we mostly renounce materialistic things. I learned that these are rather burdensome as they have to be paid for, which requires the constant scramble for money. I don't believe that materialism has ever satisfied a human being in the long run. One easily loses sight of what is really important in life and what is not."

Michael couldn't disagree.

Alexander went on. "Well, time to get back to work. Got to hurry up. I hope you have fun working with Friar Hieronymus in our wonderful library. See you at lunch then."

Friar Hieronymus and Michael set off for the monastery's main library. "Well, Michael, tell me what it is that you need to know for your research."

Michael had considered how much he should let Friar

Hieronymus know about his contract. He decided that the monk was a good man and didn't deserve to be lied to. Therefore, he told him the entire truth about the gun he was searching for and how he had stumbled across Padre de la Vega's name.

Friar Hieronymus remained silent for a moment while he unlocked the door to the library. He walked over to a big desk made from hardwood and opened one of the drawers. He pulled out two pairs of white cotton gloves and gave one pair to Michael.

The expert for firearms feared that Hieronymus might prevent him from working on such a questionable project. He turned and spoke to Michael. "My son, I have promised to help you, and I stand by my word. But please consider that Padre de la Vega most likely had a good reason for hiding that weapon so well for all that time. During my years in Rome, I was confronted with quite a few devilish tools. The Antichrist uses a lot of different devices to bring mankind's downfall. I assume you know the Bible, as Alexander told me that your parents raised you in strict Christian ways.

The Devil was always full of envy about the God-given gift of love. His entire existence he has tried to destroy love. Satan tried to seduce Jesus during his time of meditation in the desert. He wanted God's son to turn against his Father in Heaven and tried to talk Him into betraying His Heavenly Father."

Michael nodded because he knew that story in the Bible well.

"You know what really worries me, my friend? It seems as if this gun is not an ordinary weapon."

Michael looked confused. "What do you mean, Friar?"

"Well, I know that every weapon is built to kill. I'm

aware that this revolver was originally constructed for the same reason. However, what makes the difference is that this very pistol seems to be involved in cases where son turns against father. You could say their own flesh and blood executes family members after laying hands on this particular revolver. One would rather expect that weapons are used to defend the family and not to murder it, wouldn't you agree?"

Astonished, the American stared at the monk. "I have never seen it from that point of view, but you are right. This weapon seems to be indeed unusual."

"I am certain that de la Vega was a padre of one of the Spanish Benedictine monasteries. His name is typical for that region. The missionary work in Santa Fe suggests a monk from northern Spain, although it was more often the order of the Franciscan monks who were active in that area of New Mexico. When Brother Alexander told me that you are searching for facts about de la Vega, I worked a little bit ahead before you arrived here in Switzerland."

Michael was truly impressed and he slowly began to sense how much wisdom and historical knowledge had been collected behind the walls of this abbey during the past centuries.

"Since we will work together a great deal during the next few days, I suggest we address each other less formally. So, I will simply call you Michael if that is okay with you."

"That is perfect for me," Michael agreed.

"Well, Michael, you assumed Padre de la Vega returned to his home monastery. He spent the rest of his life in Spain in an abbey called Santa Domingo de Silos. It is quite an old monastery founded in 600 A.D. but was destroyed a couple of times and rebuilt again and again. It still exists and is located in a small valley of the northern Spanish province called Castille. I went through some chronicles and found a report of a Benedictine monk who traveled to different monasteries of our order in Europe during the late nineteenth century. Among other important documents he has also written a book describing different relics preserved in our monasteries. He mentioned a special item in the Abbey Santa Domingo de Silos. Let's read it together. It is written in Latin, but I will translate it to you. The Latin language and the way they used to describe things in the old days is much different from how we speak today. But I will try to translate the text into modern language. Let's go over there to the table where I have already prepared everything."

Michael spoke sincerely. "Hieronymus, I'm really thankful for all the work and time you have already invested on my behalf."

"Michael, studying books is never work for me but an enrichment, and I'm grateful that I'm allowed to work with all these treasures from different centuries. Besides, I enjoy working on a different task. It's a nice change from reading chorales or saving old Bibles from decay all the time."

They sat down at the table and Friar Hieronymus pulled a heavy leather-bound book closer. Reverently, Michael looked down at the pages made from thick parchment paper. Line after line had been beautifully written with a quill. Michael put on his cotton gloves, as he knew that these books were worth a fortune and had to be protected.

"Here it says that Padre de la Vega returned to Spain in the year 1894. Like I mentioned before, he returned after building a successful mission and church community, despite the more powerful Franciscan order in New Mexico. The monk who wrote this book reports that de la Vega was the protector of a specific relic which he kept in the monastery of Santa Domingo de Silos. He also reconfirms that this item was brought to Europe from the new world by the Padre himself. What really surprised me was the following chapter," Friar Hieronymus remarked. He bent his head to the book and read.

> During all my travels through different abbeys of our order of Saint Benedict I came across a rich collection of different holy relics. The one I stumbled across in Santo Domingo de Silos astonished me more than anything other.
>
> For the first time I was able to see a tool that did not speak of God's ways or his martyrs but rather of the evil work of Lucifer himself.
>
> Padre de la Vega had brought this devilish tool from the New World and warned his abbot and brothers that it held a curse by the doing of Satan. He implored his abbot and the entire community that this item should be kept locked away in the sacred building of God and that no one should be permitted to pass this item into the wrong hands.
>
> The custodian of the secret archives of Santo Domingo told me that the order decided to bury the relic together with Padre de la Vega after he died.
>
> According to de la Vega, the relic had been named by its last victim. Therefore, it was registered in the monastery's archives under the name *Arma del Diablo*, the Weapon of Satan.
>
> Unlike all the holy items collected in our countless churches we remain silent about this one. The Benedictine order

needs to make sure that it is never worshipped. This is a rather atypical thing, if one considers that all our relics are displayed for worldwide viewing.

According to his community, de la Vega had been a faithful man of the Bible and a reliable follower of God. He guards this evil item in the crypt under the church's altar. May God reward him for this in eternity. He won one battle against Lucifer. Strangely, he told his abbot that only the Archangel who won against Satan a long time ago, might be able to destroy the curse of the Arma del Diablo."

Friar Hieronymus stopped reading and leaned back in his chair. He studied Michael's pale face. "Sounds very unusual, doesn't it?"

Michael nodded. He knew of some stories about relics that were displayed to the public in the major churches worldwide. He had his doubts about the authenticity of some of them. It was an open secret that during medieval times many forgeries appeared. But he had never come across an item that had been hidden from the worshippers. Neither had Michael ever heard of a relic identified as evil and dangerous.

Michael said, "According to this chronicle the weapon might be still in the monastery of Santa Domingo de Los Silos, correct?"

"I would think so. But don't forget, we're talking about an event that took place more than one hundred years ago. I think it's more important to ask yourself if this weapon should be found? Wouldn't it be safer if the gun remained locked away in that sacred place?" Friar Hieronymus added seriously, "It is highly unusual that the relic is locked away like that. Let's face it, this is not a holy item, but the opposite."

Michael pressed the Friar. "But according to this text there seems to be a way to destroy the power of this weapon, or did I misunderstand?"

"You are referring to the remark about the Archangel, am I right?"

Michael nodded. Friar Hieronymus stood and walked to the wall on the opposite side of the library where he positioned a wooden ladder closer to the shelves in front of him. He climbed to the top shelf and pulled out a small, black book. A few dust mites danced through the rays of sunshine passing through the leaded glass windows.

Michael rushed to the ladder to take the book from Hieronymus' hand so he could climb down safely. As soon as Hieronymus stood on the floor, he took the black book from Michael and walked over to the table to open it. He flipped through the pages and stopped at a drawing showing the picture of a fighting Angel. The colors were rich as if the drawing had been done a few days ago. Red, gold and blue were the dominant colors.

"This is the story of the angel whom God ordered to expel another angel named Satan from heavenly Paradise. To strengthen the angel's power God gave him his own scepter to use in the fight. Satan was guilty of the sin of Pride because he wanted to be like God and didn't accept God's superiority over him. The good angel did as his heavenly father ordered and chased Satan out of Paradise and down to Earth. From that day on God's champion was known as the Archangel Michael. When you translate the name from Hebrew to our modern language it means that 'one who is like God.'"

Michael exchanged a glance with Friar Hieronymus, thinking that was the meaning of his own name, and wondering if he could ever live up to it.

The monk went on. "The other angel named Satan had to stay on Earth and was never allowed to return to Paradise. Instead of regretting his sins, he became evil and filled with hate. Nowadays we know him under the names Satan, Lucifer, the Devil and many more. He appears in countless images and myths. Numerous monks of all orders have tried to paint him according to the legends and stories told throughout the centuries."

The Friar's story was familiar to Michael, but he'd never heard such a learned man of the church tell it. He hadn't known the translation of his own name before.

"In some paintings you may see him as a snake or a dragon and in others as an ugly monster. From time to time, you may come across a portrait showing him as a human being."

Michael took the opportunity to express his opinion of the talk about angels and devils. "So I reckon that Padre de la Vega assumed that only Archangel Michael, whose existence isn't actually proven, is the one who can destroy the evil power of the gun. Is that right?"

"I would think so. But don't imagine Archangel Michael as a heavenly creature with wings. He could appear as a human being provided with protection and power by God so that he would be strong enough to fight Satan."

"Okay, let's assume that the gun is still in the abbey of Santo Domingo de Silos. Would it be possible to buy it from the order there?"

Friar Hieronymus shook his head. "This is a question I cannot answer. On one hand, it would disrespect the last will of de la Vega if the Spanish brothers sold it. On the other hand, they are most likely in financial difficulties as are most of our monasteries these days. I would say chances are 50/50. However, to achieve access to the weapon de la Vega's bones would have to be removed from the crypt. That is, if it didn't already happen a couple of years ago."

When the Swiss monk saw Michael's puzzled face, he explained what he meant. "In all monasteries we have a limited number of burial niches in the crypts. In case one of our brothers dies, and we don't have free space in the crypt we have to remove the bones of the monk who has been buried there the longest."

Friar Hieronymus explained to Michael that every abbey has a vault cellar or perhaps a chapel where the monks place the bones and skulls of brothers remaining from centuries past. There was a good chance that Padre de la Vega's remains had already been placed in the bone chapel of the monastery. After all, the good man died over hundred years ago.

Michael scratched his chin. "Ah, now I understand. The question is, how do I proceed from here? I found out some important details but I'm afraid that an American weapons expert wouldn't be welcomed in a Spanish monastery, even without the language barrier. Here it's a different story since my cousin Alexander is a member of your community and many of you speak English."

Hieronymus studied the features of the young man as he thought about it. "That could be difficult indeed, but who knows, maybe your purpose is one you don't expect. It could be that you are meant to find that gun, not to bring it to a rich collector but rather to destroy its curse."

The Friar turned in his chair to look Michael directly in the eyes. "I think we should make as much use as we can of the time you spend here in Switzerland. Maybe we can find out what's written in the archives of Santo Domingo de Silos. There might be a hint about how the power of the revolver can be destroyed. There has to be some truth behind the story, otherwise it wouldn't have scared the wits out of that Spanish padre. None of us monks would travel with a deadly weapon and we're even less likely to be buried with one. He must have had a powerful reason to do so. Maybe we can get in touch with the monastery in Castille. It's time for lunch and mass. Let's meet tomorrow morning at the same time in front of the library. Until then, I will search for a couple of documents connected to the case."

Michael smiled warmly at the friar. "I thank you from the bottom of my heart, Hieronymus. You are of such great help for me." But the Friar shrugged his shoulders and smiled. "It is fun to be a detective for a change."

They left the wonderous hall together, the monk carefully locking the external double doors. Then he waved at Michael and walked toward the church.

Michael returned to his guest room where he picked up his messenger bag, leaving the building through the side entrance. He walked across the plaza, straight to the little coffee shop where he ordered an espresso and a piece of the delicious walnut pie which was the specialty of the area.

While he enjoyed the sweet treat, he thought about the discoveries of the past few hours. He had no choice but to travel to Spain and seek access to the chronicles belonging to the abbey of Santa Domingo de Silos. Maybe Friar Hieronymus could put in a good word for him. The Spanish monastery belonged to the same order, and although they may not know the Friar personally, other Benedictines would have a good reputation.

Michael checked his mobile phone and typed a short message with warm greetings to his parents. He considered sending a report to his client Conway as well but his gut feeling told him to wait before revealing too much too early. Michael decided to continue his research until he could report a more impressive result. Besides he didn't really like the man and wasn't keen about being in touch with him. However, he had to admit that this contract was very profitable.

The good-looking American walked across the street to a small jewelry store and selected a simple, yet elegant Swiss watch for his father.

As he turned to leave, he remembered that his parents would celebrate their 50th wedding anniversary soon. Therefore, he bought a matching lady's watch for his mom. It was a special gift and thanks to the large variety and reasonable prices Michael was able to buy both without busting his budget. He was thrilled about giving them each a special present. Of course, he had to admit that this purchase was only possible due to the well-paying job he was working on at present.

Whistling a cheerful melody, he walked back through the gate of the monastery. The paper bag from the Swiss jeweler swung proudly from his arm as he returned to the guest room where he put the precious parcel in his suitcase. He had no fear that anything would be stolen here.

Since he still had time left before dinner and since the sun shone high in the sky, he spontaneously decided to explore the other side of the huge abbey complex. He knew there was a horse stable off the southeast corner of the monastery grounds.

One of the monks had told him that Einsiedeln raised a nearly extinct breed of Swiss horse called Marstall. He

had missed being around horses from his ranch upbring-
ing since moving to the city, and he was thrilled to hear
he could see an unusual breed. As he walked happily
alongside the different paddocks, some of the horses
curiously and trustingly approached him and enjoyed
having their ears scratched.

They were beautiful and robust animals. When Michael
entered the stable, he was taken by surprise. It had been
recently renovated and impressed him considerably. Each
stall was large and clean, and the entire stable was well
organized. Swallows flew through the open gates and above
the heads of the horses as they were munched on fresh hay.

The young American was more and more fascinated
by the microcosm of this monastery. The place was far
from what he had expected it to be as an example of a
religious building founded over one thousand years ago
and rebuilt three hundred years ago. As the heart of the
abbey, the church was a stunning example of baroque
architecture and a repository of incredible art treasures.
The monastery had its own cattle farm, a wine cellar, a
riding stable end a modern sawmill which provided heat
for most of the complex.

Michael felt that this location was not only a place for
worship but also an institution where centuries of wisdom,
deep reflection on philosophy, and tranquility had created
a hallowed world as well as a successful enterprise.

To his astonishment, despite the fact he had only been
in Switzerland for two days, the stress of California had
melted away. Einsiedeln was a spiritual haven.

After dinner, Alexander and Michael walked over to
the historical mill that was located next to the old work-
shops. Alexander stepped in front to climb the narrow,
wooden staircase.

The old mill had been remodeled into a cozy traditional lounge with an old-fashioned fireplace. A wooden corner bench and a weighty table invited visitors to sit.

Much to Michael's joy Alexander produced two bottles of Bavarian beer from the pockets of his robes and winked at him. The bottles carried the label of another monastery in Andechs, Bavaria which was famous for its brewery and located close to Munich in South Germany.

The two men enjoyed their conversation about their youth and their families. "You know, Alexander, I have always asked myself how in the world can a young man join a monastic order and sacrifice all worldly goods? There were times I couldn't understand your decision at all."

Alexander smiled. "Don't think that there weren't days I felt doubtful about my decision. Living in a monastery isn't easy. Especially where I'm stationed at the church gate, I'm constantly confronted with worldly problems on a daily base. It's our duty to comfort the people who seek pastoral consolation. You wouldn't believe what kind of sins people sometimes confess within our walls. We have heard everything from betrayal to robbery and even murder."

When he saw the shocked expression on his cousin's face, Alexander nodded. "You know, it's easier to confess to your priest that you killed a person than going to the police and admitting your crime there. Our congregants know that we have to follow the secrecy of the confessional. We cannot harm them or arrest them. All we can do is hope that they regret their sins and try to become better people. Perhaps even face the consequences. In most cases that's wishful thinking though."

"Have you ever thought about returning to a life outside these walls, Alexander?"

"Yes, indeed I did. But to be honest, I doubt I would be happy with a life in the so-called normal world. Most people think we sacrifice and miss things because we live as monks without material possessions. But if you analyze our lives, you will realize that we don't want for anything and that we are perhaps even richer than most folks. We don't chase money and we don't search for the meaning of life in worldly possessions. We have everything we need. See, Michael, I have a roof above my head, clothes, food, endless knowledge to learn, friendship, care… yes, even good health insurance." He laughed heartily. "We can even travel and have almost four weeks of vacation."

Alexander ticked off all the worldly problems he avoided by living the monastic life. He didn't have to worry about paying a home mortgage or a car payment. He didn't have to be concerned about a proper education for his children or whether his wife would leave him.

Michael's cousin continued to recount the advantages of giving his life to God. "I don't have to play a role pretending to be someone I'm not because I know God accepts me with all my flaws and failures, and it doesn't make any difference to him if I'm rich or poor. In case I get sick, I know that my brothers here will take care of me. And the day that I die, they will be by my side, and God will protect and welcome my soul."

"I agree with you, Alexander. Your life isn't complicated. I believe those of us out there are the ones who turn it into a rocky road, hard to travel. I would have never thought I would say this, but I may envy your life a little bit. You're living a special life here, and after only two days I recognize the strong solidarity in your community. I sometimes wonder—do you ever fight?"

"Of course, we do. Our abbot always says that all of us

below God's throne are only human beings and therefore hell- bound for failure."

A smile crossed Alexander's lips. "By the way, Friar Hieronymus told me that your research has been quite successful. I'm glad your stay with us has helped you with this project. I appreciate that you told him the truth about your motive for the research. He deserves honesty."

"He is an impressive personality and highly educated. Your library is a dream come true. I'm considering returning someday soon to stay here for a couple of weeks to study and gather inner strength and peace."

Alexander waved his hand, indicating the whole of the monastery. "You can be assured that you are welcome here anytime. Friar Hieronymus has gut feelings about people, and he says that you are a good human being."

Michael's cousin stood. "Well, I think we should call it a day as the bells will wake us tomorrow morning at 5:00 a.m., and it's going to be another day of *ora et labora* for me."

Michael joined his cousin's laughter and tried to stifle a yawn.

The following morning Michael met with the Benedictine librarian again. Hieronymus expected him and waved a piece of paper when Michael entered the amazing library.

"Good morning, Michael. I have great news for you. Sit down at the table please." A thick book lay open in front of them. Michael studied the pencil drawing of an impressive abbey.

"This is the monastery of Santo Domingo de Silos," Hieronymus explained. I emailed Padre José. He manages the archives of that monastery in Spain, and he already answered my mail."

Baffled, Michael looked over at Friar Hieronymus. It

seemed that the librarian was having fun investing time and work in this unusual case. Michael couldn't have wished for a better support person by his side.

"Padre José reconfirmed that Padre de la Vega is indeed buried in Santo Domingo de Silos. Just as I assumed, his remains were placed in the Chapel of Bones many years ago. When I asked him if a certain relic was buried with him, he answered carefully and hesitatingly, but he finally confirmed that as well. He mentioned that he would like to talk more about it, but he insists on meeting you face to face for that purpose. You need to understand that the Benedictines in Santo Domingo de Silos live a much more isolated lifestyle compared to ours here in Switzerland."

Michael scratched his chin thoughtfully. "So, it's really true. The story about de la Vega and the revolver really took place. This is absolutely crazy. The problem is that Padre José and the other Spanish monks will surely not be as open and talkative to me. Besides, my Spanish is barely good enough to order food and a café con leche. How annoying. Now that I'm so close to my goal I will probably have to give up."

The Friar remained silent and studied Michael's face. After a brief moment he spoke to his American guest. "Michael, I'm still not convinced that this weapon should be found but I will not try to talk you out of it. Instead, I suggest that we try to find out the entire story. I thought about it all morning and agree with you that most likely you would not get access to the archives nor the burial chapel in Spain. Therefore, I decided to accompany you on this mission."

Michael was sure that his ears had played a trick on him. Puzzled he looked at the man sitting next to him. But Hieronymus was smiling.

"My dear friend, even we have a certain allowance of vacation days per year. Our abbot complained that I've been hiding behind my books too much lately, and that I still have a whole heap of vacation days left over from last year. I spoke with him this morning and he already agreed that I can travel with you. The monastery we want to visit is close to a town called Burgos and therefore right on the Way of St. James' pilgrim path.

Once we're done with our research in Santo Domingo, I would continue the Way of Saint James to the Cathedral of Santiago de Compostela. I haven't been there in ages and would love to see it again. A bit of hiking and going on pilgrimage doesn't hurt, even if you are a monk. All we need to do is to find a matching flight and book a rental car."

Michael sat there, feeling thunderstruck. "You would really do this for me, Hieronymus?"

"Of course, I would. I'm really excited to find out more about this unusual story. Besides I'm curious to see the library of my Spanish colleagues."

"All right then, I will take care of booking the flights and the rental car. How soon can you leave, Hieronymus?"

"Day after tomorrow, under the condition that we find a suitable connecting flight. In any case, I have to be back in Switzerland six days later. But flight times are short. That's the advantage how small Europe is, compared to your huge country."

Both men left the library and parted. Michael returned to his guest room where he picked up his laptop and walked over to his favorite coffee shop across the plaza. While he waited for his cappuccino, he logged into the app for international flights.

He found a flight from Zurich to the Spanish city of Bilbao which was less than one- and one-half hours by car from their final destination.

Without hesitation he used his credit card and booked the flight for him and a return ticket for Friar Hieronymus. It was unlikely he would be granted access to the Spanish monastery's archives without a Benedictine monk by his side. Anyway, it would be nice to have a cordial traveling companion.

The following day both men kept busy preparing for their journey. While Friar Hieronymus quickly gathered a few Swiss souvenirs for his Spanish Benedictine brothers, Michael hiked to a small lake that lay nestled near the town of Einsiedeln. Michael marveled at the beautiful scenery. He noticed parts of the Swiss Alps still wore their snow caps in the background. The panorama was simply gorgeous.

Meanwhile he had bought a whole bag of the chocolate bars his mother desperately wanted. He was relieved that he could stuff all his purchases into his large suitcase for his return flight to the United States.

Brother Alexander and Michael spent their last evening together since Michael planned to fly back to the U.S. from Spain. He would miss his cousin and hoped that Alexander would visit him in Montana someday soon.

The days in the Swiss monastery had left Michael thoughtful about the sense of solidarity and respect among the monks. The aura of the place reminded him of his parents' home.

During the short hike to the lake, he decided to build his new home in Montana sooner rather than later. He felt the sudden urge to escape hectic and money-driven California.

Alexander was very pleased he had made that decision and reminded Michael that he would be welcomed in Einsiedeln any time. But he also warned Michael of the dangers connected to the profession of weapons expert.

He reminded him of the fact that not everyone handled weapons with common sense.

Next morning Friar Hieronymus and Michael Kent were ready for departure. They loaded their suitcases into the waiting taxi which would take them to the train station.

Alexander hugged his cousin and once again emphasized how nice it would be if they could see each other soon again. Then the monk wished both men a successful and safe journey.

A sense of melancholy descended on Michael when he saw the impressive facade of the Swiss monastery disappear in the rearview mirror of the cab.

CHAPTER TWELVE

***

SANTO DOMINGO DE SILOS—SPAIN

Friar Hieronymus was excited about the journey ahead. At first Michael hardly recognized the man when he came around the corner dressed in civilian clothes.

Hieronymus's slim frame sported a fashionable outfit of faded denims and a sports shirt with a blue and green block print. A blue backpack completed the outfit. If Michael hadn't known better, he would have never expected the man to be a member of the clergy.

They took the train to the Zurich airport, arriving there forty minutes later. Michael picked up a luggage trolley and loaded both suitcases onto it, checking them both through to Bilbao. At first Hieronymus protested since Michael had paid for his ticket as well, but once Michael explained it was a gift for all the support, Hieronymus had given him he accepted the present after a moment's hesitation.

The two men enjoyed a lively conversation during the short flight. They exchanged anecdotes about their lives, and before long they felt the descent of the plane over the city of Bilbao.

Once they landed, Michael picked up the rental car and they packed their luggage into its trunk. Fortunately, he had booked a car with a navigation system. They enjoyed their drive through the scenic high plateau of the north Castilian country. After a while, they stopped in a small town and drank a typical Spanish café con leche. The two men felt as if they were on vacation and were able to forget their dangerous mission. In the early evening, they arrived at the monastery of Santa Domingo de Silos near the town of Burgos.

Hieronymus rang the bell at the gate of the abbey. To Michael's surprise, his Swiss friend introduced them to the elder monk who had opened the door in perfect Spanish. He explained that Padre José was expecting them. The Spanish monk motioned them inside and told Friar Hieronymus that he expected them also. He led them to a wing where a few modest guest rooms were located.

As they walked behind the brother, Michael remarked, "Golly, Hieronymus, I had no idea that you speak Spanish so well."

The Swiss librarian grinned at him. "Oh, you'd be surprised. Most of us speak at least two languages fluently, some of us three or four. There are advantages to living at an international pilgrimage location, you see. And don't forget I have daily access to thousands of books."

"Your linguistic skills are another reason I'm grateful you came with me. I'd have been pointing and grunting."

Both men placed their luggage in their guest rooms and Friar Hieronymus dressed in his monk's cassock again. They asked another Spanish Benedictine for directions to the dining hall, where they were welcomed warmly when they found it.

Padre José awaited them there. Friar Hieronymus introduced Michael Kent, and the Spanish monk promised to take them to the archives the following morning. After finishing dinner both guests withdrew early since they were tired from their long day of travels. However, Friar Hieronymus attended evening prayers first, as a faithful man of the Bible.

The following morning both men got up early, and after a plain breakfast, they accompanied Padre José to the library of the Santa Domingo de Silos Monastery.

The hall was much less ornate than the one in Einsiedeln, but the vaulted ceiling and the chiseled sandstone pillars were impressive. The building was much older than Friar Hieronymus's, as it hadn't been destroyed as recently. Even this library held a substantial number of historical books. More and more Michael felt in awe by the collection of wisdom within the timeworn walls of the Benedictine order.

Padre José turned toward Michael. The Spanish Benedictine spoke quite a bit of English, although he had a strong accent, and Michael had to listen carefully. The monk didn't hold back, reporting that the remains of Padre de la Vega were located in the Chapel of Bones among those of others who died many years ago. He promised to show them that chapel later.

The three men sat around a huge wooden desk which stood in the middle of the library. "Is it okay for you if I call you Michael?"

"Of course, Padre José. No need to be formal with me."

"Very well. I want to tell you the story of Padre de la Vega. He was a missionary in that town now known as Santa Fe, New Mexico. When he returned from the Old World, he wanted to spend his last years here because it is his home. According to the chronicles he came back not only visibly aged but also turned inward. He spent his time alone, studying whatever kinds of holy documents and Bibles he could lay hands on. He also wrote countless documents himself."

Padre José studied the desktop for a moment. "As you may know, we not only believe in God and the Holy Church, but also in Satan and evil that walks among mankind. In Padre de la Vega's case, the acceptance of Lucifer went far beyond the norm. He wrote in one of his documents that a novice convinced him of el Diablo's existence. Something happened in Santa Fe that shook his confidence deeply. He returned from the new world and, to our astonishment, brought a relic of evil into this monastery."

Michael slid nervously to the edge of his chair. "Do you know what kind of relic that was?" he asked, unable to control his curiosity.

Padre José remained silent for a moment, but then he nodded slowly. "We know indeed. It was a revolver, Michael."

Friar Hieronymus and the firearms expert exchanged a meaningful glance. Padre José leaned back in his chair and studied the two of them silently. When he spoke again his voice was barely more than a whisper. He wore a serious expression, the corners of his mouth turned down.

"I think it's time that the two of you tell me the truth regarding what this is all about and why you are looking for that gun. There are more firearms in this world besides this one, and God would surely not appreciate any of them. So why does it have to be this particular revolver?"

Friar Hieronymus didn't say a word. It was Michael Kent's decision to share what he wanted with the Spanish Benedictine monk. Since Michael was an honest man, he told Padre José about his job and the results of their research so far. He emphasized that the story wasn't only about a six-shooter belonging to a famous outlaw during pioneer days, but that he was most likely looking for the prototype of this model. Therefore, the gun would be worth a lot of money.

He told the tragic tale of Ludwig Schmied, the designer and builder of the pistol. Padre José interrupted Michael and asked if Ludwig had constructed the weapon all alone. The unexpected question confused the weapon expert. Why was this important for Padre José to know? But despite wondering about it, Michael described the entries in Ludwig's diary mentioning the eerie stranger who had given him drawings of essential construction details.

"Did he describe that strange man?" Padre José wanted to know.

"He wrote that he had been a weird-looking man with dark, piercing eyes and black hair who seemed to know a lot about Ludwig before he ever met him. When I read the diary, I got the impression that the gunsmith feared him. Nevertheless, he allowed the stranger to influence him in the worst possible way."

"I understand," the Spanish monk nodded, knitting his brows thoughtfully. Michael had no clue why this detail was so important for Padre José. The Spanish Benedictine abruptly stood and walked to one of the countless bookshelves. He grabbed a leather-bound book and brought it back to the table. It looked old and well-used. A thick leather cord held it together.

Padre José opened the book. He flipped through the pages seemingly searching for something specific. The other two men waited patiently. He grasped the book in both hands and struggled to read the English text. Curious, Michael leaned forward.

"The text that I'm reading now is part of a letter which de la Vega received weeks after returning from Santa Fe."

Dear Padre de la Vega,

We all hope you're doing well and are glad that you arrived safely back in your home country of Spain, according to your letter.

Your church community misses you greatly. I'm writing this letter today because of some strange events that took place here after you left.

A few days ago, a weird visitor came to see me in my office. I admit I have come across numerous questionable characters during my years as law dog, but this stranger was an outstanding example of a cold-blooded individual. I had never seen him before. His eerie appearance was emphasized by his black hair and the fact that he was completely dressed in black clothes.

Strangely, he wanted to buy the six-shooter young Hernandez used to shoot his father. You surely understand that I was confused about the fact that a stranger to our town even knew about the Colt. He must have heard about it in one of the countless saloons here.

I told him that the revolver was no longer in my office, but it seemed as if he hadn't heard me at all. He continued to offer me money and to be honest Padre I was truly shocked about the unbelievable amount of 500 silver dollars he wanted to pay for that barking iron.

Think about it. How many good things could have been done in town or for your church with all those silver coins? Anyway, I explained that Josef's spiritual father had taken the gun with him to a safe depository where he most likely keeps it.

You should have seen his face, Padre. His dark eyes threw daggers at me and his face looked really somber. He cursed worse than any man I have ever heard in my living days and due to my Christian faith, I don't want to repeat his words in this letter.

I still don't understand his behavior. Any man knows there are enough firearms out here which can be bought for a percentage of the amount he offered me. I admit, Padre, I was sure glad when he left my office and I hope he never comes back. I'm relieved that you are back in Europe safely. The Southwest is a dangerous territory to live in.

You know me well enough to understand that I hardly fear anything in life but I'm not ashamed to admit that I was somewhat scared of this man, and I cannot even explain why.

Warmest Regards,
Sheriff Willbury

Padre José looked at Hieronymus and Michael. He kept the book open in front of him. Michael returned his gaze. "Wow. Looks like I am not the first one who to search for that gun. Apparently, the Colt 45 was an object of desire even 100 years ago."

The Spanish monk nodded, pointing to the book. "Michael, you told me that your collector gave you Padre de la Vega's diary when you met him. This book is the second diary that our good padre wrote after returning to this monastery. The unusual part is that he always claimed that the first book which described his years as a missionary disappeared during his journey back to Spain. He never found out who took it from his trunk while he traveled across the ocean. If he hadn't worn the weapon strapped to his body, it would most likely have been stolen, too. However, in this second diary, he describes his last conversation with the young Hernandez before the poor fellow was executed one more time."

Again, the Spanish padre pulled the book closer and started to read:

> "Josef confessed his sins. He seemed more prepared to face his destiny than I. When I was about to leave his cell, he grabbed my arm and told me he has an important task for me. He urged me to take that terrible revolver he used to shoot his father and hide it somewhere far away to make sure it could never get into the wrong hands again.
>
> Then Josef told me something that he didn't confess to anybody else during his trial. He claimed that a stranger had been in the house when he shot his father. Josef described the man. According to him that stranger stood in a corner and observed everything but didn't try to stop

his father from beating his mother. Rather the opposite was the case. Josef saw the stranger smiling.

When I asked the boy who this man was, he shook his head and said, "I have never seen him in town before, Padre, but he told me to shoot at my father. I heard his voice in my head but strangely his lips didn't move. He urged me again and again to do something, or my Pa would kill my mom. I hadn't even thought about the revolver, but the stranger told me that I held the tool to stop that terrible beating and to save her."

I admit that I wondered if my novice had lost his mind and I was sure that he was still in a state of shock. But then poor Josef described the stranger in a very detailed way and convinced me that he couldn't have made up such a wild tale. He knew that lies would not prevent his life from ending at the gallows.

According to him the stranger was a tall man with black hair and piercing dark eyes. Josef described them as pieces of "cold coal." He said the man was dressed in black from head to toe and his lips smiled sardonically. Joseph emphasized that he was scared of the man but nevertheless had felt compelled to follow his orders. He told me that the man had some sort of control over his own willpower. When I asked him what all this had to do with the gun, Josef whispered, "*Esta es el arma del diablo,*"— "*It is the weapon of the Devil.*"

Michael stared at the book, horrified, sensing that there was pure evil behind that story. He wasn't aware that he crossed himself. Friar Hieronymus wore an extremely worried expression as well. But Padre José wasn't finished reading, so he continued with the story.

> "I promised the youthful convict I would keep the weapon until I could take it to a sacred place and lock it away for good. Josef begged for a piece of paper and a pencil from the Sheriff. When I asked him what he needed it for he told me that he had to write down his legacy. I wouldn't withhold fulfilling the last will for a young man who would die soon and called the Sheriff. I insisted that I needed some paper and a lead pencil. I wanted to give him the paper but when I returned to the cell, Josef Hernandez had his eyes closed. At first, I thought he had fallen asleep or that he might be praying. But a few moments later he took the piece of paper and put it on the floor.
>
> One can imagine my surprise when the boy didn't write anything but drew a picture. He was truly artistically gifted. It didn't take long before the portrait of a man emerged from his rapid strokes with the pencil.
>
> He didn't show me the portrait but rolled the paper up and gave it to me. I will never forget Josef Hernandez's words. They confused me and yes, even shocked me. "Padre, please never give

that horrible Colt to any man or boy and
don't ever sell it. There are only two men
who can break the power and spell of this
weapon. One of them is responsible for
the revolver's existence. Only when the
gun returns to his very hands it will lose
its deadly power because the circle will be
complete. The other man knows the tools
of calamity well and he has beaten the
master of perdition once before."

Carefully the Spanish monk closed the book. An eerie
silence filled the room. Rays of sunlight streamed through
the leaded glass windows. It was a beautiful day in northern Spain, but Michael's skin had gone cold, goosebumps
rising on his arms.

What was this prophecy about? Who were the two men
young Hernandez mentioned? Did the gun really possess
some sort of evil power beyond the fact that it could kill?
Was that really possible?

Question after question stormed through Michael's
mind. Finally, Friar Hieronymus broke the silence. "Before
we get too crazy with our speculations, I suggest we search
for proof that certain items have indeed carried some sort
of curse in the past. However, I'm afraid that this will be
time-consuming research. I guess the gun is still in this
monastery, isn't it?"

Padre José remained silent, so Hieronymus continued,
"That boy in Santa Fe spoke prophetically of two men
who would be capable of destroying the spell of the Colt.
We need to find out who he meant. And there is another
question. Who was that stranger Josef mentioned when he
spoke with Padre de la Vega? It almost sounds as if it was

the same man who showed up at the Sheriff's Office few weeks later to buy that horrible gun."

"Really sounds like it, doesn't it?" remarked Michael. He was unusual pale, and the story burdened him more than he admitted. *What have I gotten myself into*?

Padre José checked his wristwatch and suggested that the two visitors take a walk through the monastery's garden to relax. Then they could all meet again for lunch. "I think a bit of fresh air would help digest this new information. That okay for you, Michael?"

The two visitors stepped into the inner courtyard of the monastery. A loggia, or open hallway with a series of archways surrounded the courtyard. Its ceiling was supported by countless stone pillars. A perfectly kept garden with cypresses, box tree hedges and a big fountain in its middle awaited them. Stone benches invited the visitors to sit down, relax, or simply enjoy the calming sound of the gurgling water and the happy chirping of the birds. The place had a meditative atmosphere. Both men sat on the stone bench closest to the fountain. They were visibly worried about the things they had just heard.

"Michael, I know you have to fulfill this contract, but to be honest with you, I don't think that this Colt 45 should be delivered to this collector."

Michael nodded. "I'll lose lots of money if I don't fulfil the obligations of this job. However, I'll have to decide what to do once we finish our research and know more about the case. Don't get me wrong, I understand your concerns and I'm really thankful because I would have never gotten this far without your help, Hieronymus."

The Swiss friar shrugged his shoulders. "You know, Michael, I believe that there are no coincidences in life and people who are meant to meet for a specific reason will get together one way or another. God delegates everything on this planet and I'm one hundred percent certain that he sent you to Einsiedeln for a good reason. Well, let's go back inside. I need to spend a bit time with my Benedictine brothers if you don't mind."

While Friar Hieronymus passed the rest of the day with the monks of the abbey, Michael stayed in his guest room going through all the notes he had taken. Padre José continued searching through the documents in the library.

Again, and again, Michael thought about the prophecy the young Hernandez had made. *The man who created the gun is the only one who can break its spell.* Michael was confused about this, and he tried to understand what Josef Hernandez meant by that.

He leaned back in the wooden chair, and as always when he was thinking hard, he talked to himself. "Okay, let's see. Ludwig constructed the gun. That is a known fact. But that means that the Colt 45 would have to be returned to Ludwig Schmied. That is impossible since that poor chap was buried behind the walls of the cemetery. I wonder if that cemetery and the wall around it still exists after all these years. I bet my Italian coffee that most likely a shopping center or an apartment complex was erected there by now."

Michael ran his fingers through his hair in despair. He was close to calling the whole thing off. Why not let Conway search for the dang revolver himself? Of course, Michael was aware that even if Conway found the weapon, he would still pursue him as an expert to certify its authenticity. That would be easy if the serial number was still visible, at least clearly enough to identify the gun as the prototype.

Michael checked his watch. An idea crossed his mind and he dialed Frieda's number in Fredericksburg. She picked up on the second ring.

"Hello Frieda, it's me, Michael Kent."

"Oh, hi Michael. What a pleasant surprise."

"Frieda, I'm calling you from overseas on my mobile phone, so I'll have to keep this call short. I just have one question." The elderly lady laughed.

"I'll be darned, you get around more than an American Airlines pilot, don't you? Okay, fire your question at me, cowboy. What can I do for you?"

"You told me that Ludwig was buried in his hometown outside the cemetery wall, correct?"

Frieda remained silent for moment, and Michael wondered if the connection had been interrupted. At last, she answered his question. "Originally that was the case, as the church didn't allow a person who committed suicide to be laid to rest in hallowed ground. But to be honest, Ludwig's mother never got past the breakup of the family and the fact that her youngest son was thrown out of the house.

She loved her youngest the best. She bribed the undertaker to excavate Ludwig's body a few days afterward and to bury him secretly in the family's mausoleum. She wanted to make sure that the family was united again in death. Sadly, she never overcame the tragedy, she became very ill and died only two years after the drama took place in their house. She passed away overnight from heart failure."

Frieda gave Michael the location of the mausoleum in Cedar Hill Cemetery in Hartford. She imparted that she was the last living relative and pays the annual cemetery fee which covers the monument's upkeep. She mentioned she had last visited two years previously. "Michael, why do you ask?"

"I can't tell you too much yet, but it is possible that I will need your help once again. I know this might sound shocking to you, but chances are good that I will need you to accompany me to Ludwig's grave and allow me to enter the family's mausoleum."

Michael heard Frieda gasp. He went on. "I assure you that I would never harm Ludwig's reputation or that of your family. Rather the opposite is the case since I might have found a way to repair the memory of the tragic events that happened in the house of your relative. As soon as I know more, and I'm back in the United States, I'll contact you. You really helped me with the diary. I thank you for being so honest. We will definitely speak to each other soon."

Frieda's voice relaxed. "You can call me anytime, Michael. I trust you, and I know that the history of my family is in good hands. I hope you have a successful time in Europe and a safe journey back home."

Michael decided to go to bed early to get ready for the next day. Since he couldn't fall asleep right away, he glanced around the sparsely furnished room. A wooden cross hung on the wall opposite from his bed, and a small desk stood under the window, holding a Bible, waiting to be read. On impulse, he picked up the book of the holy word and took it back to the bed.

He opened the Bible, searching for the paragraph that described how Satan was expelled from Paradise. Many years ago, his mother had read the story to him, but Michael remembered only parts of it. His mother had always loved this legend, and thanks to the story, Michael had received his first name. He read the pages that described how an angel named Lucifer was adored as the bringer of light in heaven. But his pride and greed had no limit and Lucifer tried to equate himself with God. The creator of mankind was furious about it and tendered the scepter of power to another angel, giving him the order to expel Lucifer from Paradise.

Archangel Michael did as he was ordered and Lucifer, now known as Satan, was never allowed to join the other angels in Paradise again. God was pleased with the way Michael had followed his orders and therefore rewarded him with the position of Archangel.

Now he was one of the three angels that lead God's legions. Satan, who was doomed to live on Earth from then on, became the Accuser and turned his back on God. He was full of hate and anger and became God's most dangerous rival and enemy.

The firearms expert closed the Bible and put it on his nightstand. Suddenly an outrageous thought crossed his mind. He remembered the prophecy of the youthful convict Josef Hernandez. The poor fellow convinced Padre de la Vega that the revolver held a terrible curse. He told his friend that the second man who could break the spell of the Colt 45 would be someone who knows the tools of evil well. And it would be a person who has won a battle against the Master of Darkness before.

What if Josef was referring to weapons when he spoke of the tools of evil? And could it be possible that the Master of Darkness was no one less than the Devil himself?

Michael knew that according to the *Holy Bible* only two had been able to win their fight against Lucifer. One had been God's son Jesus, when he didn't succumb to Satan's temptation, and the second was Archangel Michael.

The young American didn't like it at all when he realized that he knew a lot about firearms which could be considered the devil's tools. And he was the namesake of Archangel Michael.

His mother had always assumed that he had a higher purpose in this world, but Michael had always been sure that she meant an outstanding career. But what if his destiny was a different path—one that was unimaginable?

Well Hoss, it doesn't make any sense to drive yourself crazy with speculations. We have to be patient and wait to see what we find out, then go from there. One thing I know for sure, this is the weirdest job I have ever worked in my entire professional life. Chances are I have gotten myself into a real mess this time, he thought and finally fell into an exhausted sleep.

CHAPTER THIRTEEN

***

PATER DE LA VEGA'S LEGACY

During the third day of their stay in the Spanish abbey Michael met Padre José and Friar Hieronymus in the library and told them that he was convinced that the two mentioned in Josef Hernandez's prophecy were none other than gunsmith Ludwig Schmied and Archangel Michael. He admitted that it sounded absolutely crazy, but the two men of the clergy shook their heads.

Hieronymus spoke first. "Michael, we believe everything that is written in the Bible, whether it is about Jesus being crucified, him rising from the dead, or Adam and Eve in the Garden of Eden. Do you really think that what you just said sounds too crazy for us? We committed our entire lives to the holy word, despite the fact that we have proof for only a few things written in the bible. But we have our faith, and I believe you could be right. It sounds plausible."

Hieronymus tapped his chin thoughtfully. "Ludwig was the one who created that gun. The hate and betrayal he experienced within his own family most likely opened the door for murdering his father and brother. It isn't hard to believe that this crime might have activated some sort of curse connected with that Colt 45. There's a chapter in the Bible that says evil cannot harm a man unless a human being allows evil to enter his heart. That would explain why Padre de la Vega was able to carry the weapon on his body without being taken by the curse. He had dedicated his life to God and therefore the Devil had no chance to attack his soul. I'm quite certain that Satan's tools can lose their power like Satan lost his fight against Archangel Michael if only a person is faithfully dedicated to God."

Michael rubbed the tabletop with his index finger. "Hieronymus, you've dedicated your life to God, but I haven't, so I wouldn't be immune to the curse."

The Friar didn't respond directly to Michael's comment. "Don't misunderstand me. I don't believe that Josef Hernandez or Ludwig Schmied were malign people. It rather looks like certain events in the family brought forward a specific weakness which made it possible for corruption to infect them like a terrible disease."

Padre José nodded in agreement. Michael stared at the table lost in thought. But then he looked straight into the Jose's eyes. "Considering this, it means that there is always a chance that this weapon might end up in the wrong hands, even here in this monastery. If we believe the prophecy of Hernandez, we will have to return that fateful prototype Colt back to Ludwig Schmied, a man who died over 130 years ago. Is that right?"

Friar Hieronymus agreed. "Do we have the slightest clue where Ludwig Schmied is buried? I'm afraid it will be impossible to find his grave decades after he died especially when we consider the amount of construction done in places like Connecticut since then."

"Actually, we do indeed have a clue," said Michael and told his two new friends about his phone conversation with Ludwig's only surviving relative.

Padre José smiled. "Now this is what I call good news."

"Don't call it a good day before evening has passed, my dear friend," Michael warned him. "So far we don't know if your abbot would be willing to hand over the firearm which Padre de la Vega has guarded for so many years. How do we get him to trust me, an unknown stranger? And how can we convince him to let me take the gun back to the United States to lock it into the coffin of the poor chap who rests inside the family's mausoleum?"

José spread his hands. "You might be surprised. The leader of this order is quite a modern man. I'm sure you can imagine that worldly worries about the continued existence of this monastery are his main burden these days. Our church faces the same problem worldwide—a lack of willing new novices to join our orders and clergy. In addition, the financial burden gets worse with each passing year. This abbey is over a thousand years old and despite rebuilding and regular renovations it takes a lot of money to keep it in shape. We have relics in our church that are more famous. I'm not even sure if our young abbot knows the story about Padre de la Vega and the cursed gun."

Shifting his weight, José hung an arm over the back of his chair. "As you know this relic cannot be worshiped, and he cannot expect any donation money from it. The extremely costly renovation of the church roof is something that has bothered him lately. His priority number one is to make sure that this monastery continues its existence. Maybe he would be even relieved to get rid of this terrible item. The more facts we can show him, the better the chances are going to be that he will relinquish it. In any case we have to remain honest because if something really makes him furious it is when people lie straight to his face."

Michael stroked his chin. "So, the question is, do we have enough facts to convince him that I need this gun to break a dangerous spell?"

Padre José got up and walked over to his desk. He picked up a beautifully carved wooden box and returned to the table where the other two men waited for him. Padre José removed two paper rolls from the casket and held them for moment, looking at his two visitors. "The entire length of your visit, a feeling that I had forgotten something important irritated me. One gets forgetful with increasing age. Anyway, tonight I finally remembered what it was. Padre de la Vega didn't only return to Spain with the pistol but also with this little wooden casket. Besides his diary he also kept these two drawings in it. Do you remember how Josef Hernandez asked for paper and a lead pencil after he had confessed his sins in jail?" Both men nodded to show they remembered.

"Josef must have been a very talented young man because he made a drawing of the weapon he used to shoot his father to make sure that the Sheriff would hand over the correct gun to his Benedictine friend. Despite the convict's young age he was smart enough to prevent any man from keeping the real Colt for himself to sell later while handing over a different one to Padre de la Vega. A missionary wouldn't have known the difference."

Carefully Padre José unrolled the paper and held the corners in place with two books. Astonished Michael stared at the unusually detailed drawing showing an SAA Colt 45. Although it was only a drawing the firearm looked quite threatening. The 222 serial number was clearly recognizable.

For the very first time since his decision to become
a firearms expert he felt deeply disgusted by a gun. He
couldn't say if it had to do with the tragedies connected to
the pistol or whether it was fear of the power of that specific
Colt. Above the drawing Josef Hernandez had written the
Spanish words *Arma del Diablo.*

"This one really looks like a tool of the devil, doesn't
it?" Friar Hieronymus remarked as he studied the drawing
with his brow furrowed.

Michael looked up from the drawing of the weapon.
"Padre José, in his diary de la Vega mentioned that the
boy sketched the portrait of a person. Did he draw the
stranger who was in the same room when he shot his
father, by any chance?"

Thoughtfully the Spanish monk rolled up the drawing
of the revolver and put the document aside. Instead of
answering Michael's question he took the second paper
and spread it on the table. Again, he weighed down its
corners with the two books. Since he was dressed in the
black habit and stood right in front of the table the drawing
only became visible once he stepped aside.

The moment Michael saw it he jumped up, his chair
falling over. The American gasped for air and his face
lost its healthy color. The noise caused by the falling chair
sounded like an earthquake in the silent library.

Astonished, Friar Hieronymus studied his American
friend's face. Michael looked as if he would faint any
moment. His eyes reflected pure shock. "Michael, what's
the matter?" Padre José looked puzzled as well. He didn't
understand why the firearms expert seemed panic-stricken.

At first Michael was unable to speak. *This is not possible. I am mistaken. My eyes play a nasty trick on me.*
He couldn't recall ever having felt such disorientation.

The son of the Hernandez family must have been a real artist, he thought.

Michael stared at the piece of paper in disbelief, feeling sick. The piercing black eyes of his client Gorgo Conway stared back at him.

After picking up his chair Michael sat down, his head still spinning from the shock. He trembled and looked over at the two Benedictine monks. His voice was barely more than a whisper when he said, "The man in this picture is none other than the collector who hired me to find this gun."

"Santo Dios." the Spanish monk exclaimed. Friar Hieronymus crossed himself. Even he looked pale now. "But how is that possible?" asked the librarian of Einsiedeln. "This portrait was drawn in Santa Fe in 1890, and you received this contract only a couple of weeks ago in California. Is there a chance that you might confuse Conway with that chap on the paper because Conway resembles the man in this drawing?"

But Michael shook his head vehemently. "Out of the question. This drawing could be a photo of Mr. Gorgo Conway. That's how precise the picture is."

The Spanish monk was about to roll up the drawing but stopped in midair. "Wait a minute, how did you call this man?"

"Conway, his name is Conway."

But the Benedictine shook his head. "No, no, what was his first name?"

"Well, he introduced himself as Gorgo Conway. I know it is a weird first name. I have never heard it before. Maybe he has some Russian ancestors or some Eastern European blood. That would explain his high cheekbones as well. I have no idea. In any case he looks alien and has unusual dark eyes and black hair."

The Spanish Benedictine got up and walked over to a bookshelf. He spent a few minutes with his head bent reading the spines, but at last he pulled a book off the shelf. He returned to the table and opened the well-used book.

He turned the pages to one that was marked with a red silk string. Michael realized that a list of names was written in Gothic-style letters. The heading was beautifully ornamented, as often seen in the holy books. Michael barely knew Latin words, but these were not difficult to understand. The heading read *Nomina Diaboli*, the names of the devil. Puzzled he looked at the Spanish librarian.

The monk followed the lines with his finger still clad in the white cotton glove. The names were in alphabetical order. Suddenly his index finger stopped, and he turned the book so that Michael and Hieronymus were able to read it.

"Gorgo, a name used in ancient Greek as nomenclature for Satan," Padre José read. "This could be a coincidence. But I doubt it if your client is really the same person that we saw in this portrait."

The three men remained silent and sat with knit brows. The more they found out, the more shocking the facts were. After a few minutes Friar Hieronymus spoke. "I would say it is obvious why this so-called collector named Conway has not done further research himself, although he owned Padre de la Vega's diary. If he's really the one who controlled the willpower of that boy in Santa Fe, he cannot enter any sacred building or any property that is blessed and dedicated to God. Therefore, he has to use you, Michael, to gain access to those Christian institutions which are strictly prohibited for him. Of course, this is an unbelievable thought considering the modern times we live in, but let's face it, haven't we battled evil and Satan for centuries?"

"I do believe in the existence of Lucifer just like I believe in the existence of God. The Devil is part of our biblical history. If you study the past of the dictators in this world, one is easily convinced that the Devil himself is quite active on this planet. No human being could produce such perverted lust for evil, if not for the works of the fallen angel Satan. Question is, where do we go from here?"

Padre José had listened silently. He scratched his chin, obviously lost in thought. Finally, when he started to talk, he turned toward Michael. "You mentioned that you know where this gunsmith is buried, correct?"

Michael nodded. "His last surviving relative told me that his grave is in the same city where the Colt Firearms Company is located."

Father Hieronymus pondered that thought. "I'm afraid that this terrible weapon won't be safe in this monastery in the long run. What if someday a new abbot gets rid of this relic by either selling it or throwing it away because he doesn't know the history of it? We all know that every monastery in this world lacks followers as well as financial support these days. The importance and dangerous truth behind this story might get lost over the next few decades. I believe that the only solution is to fulfill the prophecy foretold by Joseph Hernandez."

Michael interrupted. "Which means I have to try to get this Colt out of this monastery and bring it over to the United States to bury it with Ludwig Schmied's remains. But even when your abbot agrees to this, which seems rather unlikely, I would still need Frieda Miller's agreement to open that poor fellow's grave. I'm not a fool, I know how difficult it will be to convince these two people of the necessity to do so."

Padre José nodded. "In my opinion, the first step to make

this happen is to talk to the leader of our order without hiding anything. We have to tell him the truth. If you agree, I will organize a meeting for the four of us this afternoon. I'm sure that he will be relieved to get rid of this dangerous relic once he finds out who is behind its existence, and that the same being currently searches for it. He's quite young and I'm certain that he has not looked into the story of Padre de la Vega yet. I'm afraid that his predecessor has tried his best to hide the secret."

Michael looked across the table at the Swiss monk. "What do you think, Hieronymus?"

Friar Hieronymus took a deep breath. "I do believe Padre José is right. It seems to be our only chance. Unfortunately, a huge responsibility rests on your shoulders. I'm afraid it will be a race against time but not impossible. I am convinced that the weapon will lose its power the very moment it is returned to its creator, Ludwig Schmied. That will be the moment when Gorgo Conway most likely loses his interest in this Colt. The most difficult part will be to hide the fact that you've already found the gun until the moment you arrive at Ludwig's grave. You will have to be strong while you carry the weapon because you will be unprotected from it. You have to make sure that the power of the curse doesn't affect you. I'm sure this pistol is dangerous to you. Since you are an expert in firearms and fascinated by the topic it might be easy for the curse to poison you."

Hieronymus leaned forward, folding his hands on the table. "You told me that you were brought up as a good Christian. You will need all your strength to reactivate the power of your faith. It will be the only way to keep this tool of evil from tempting you like it did the others. Try not to touch it with your bare hands. It would be best if you had a member of the clergy by your side. The journey to Connecticut is the most dangerous part. Under any condition, we have to prevent your client from knowing that you carry the gun. I'm sure your life would be in grave danger if he knew. But I'm quite sure that he will lose interest in you as soon as the spell is broken. Unfortunately, you will probably lose your payment for this contract, but human life is more important than any amount of cash in this world, isn't it?"

"You're both right," said Michael. "Let me talk to the abbot. But if there is a possibility, I would like to take a look at the weapon first. I want to make sure that it's really the gun that I'm looking for. And I want to be certain I can resist its spell."

Brother José nodded, got up, and put the books back onto the shelves. He carefully rolled up the two sketches and laid them back into the small wooden casket that stood on his desk. Then the Spanish monk took the key ring and asked his two visitors to follow him.

They walked along the halls in silence, all three occupied with their own thoughts. At last, they reached the bone chapel next to the burial crypt. Niches of different sizes lined the walls, holding hundreds of skulls and bones piled high.

The front area was dominated by a small wooden prayer bench and a tall, intricate candleholder. The chapel had a peaceful atmosphere where Michael sensed the presence of all the monks who had found their final rest here.

In one of the side niches on the right a single skull and the bones of a man were placed on top of a faded velvet cloth that must have been of a rich burgundy color years ago. A beautifully carved, small trunk made from hardwood stood in the middle of these bones. Brother

José crossed himself before the tall wooden cross hanging from the ceiling at the far end of the Chapel. After saying a short prayer, he walked over to the niche and carefully picked up the wooden casket. Once he made certain that the bones were undisturbed, he tenderly put the chest down on the prayer bench.

Michael didn't dare to ask, but Padre José easily read the unspoken question on the American's face. The Benedictine whispered, "These are the remains of Padre de la Vega."

Hieronymus and Michael bent their heads in respect, and both whispered a short prayer. Michael knew that de la Vega had risked his life to hide the weapon in this sacred building just as he had promised poor Josef Hernandez before his execution. Michael stepped closer and waited nervously for Padre José to open the complicated antique lock securing the casket's lid. Padre José searched for the key among countless others on his big key ring. At last, he found a small key with an elaborate head, and inserting it into the lock, and he turned it carefully.

Michael expected the lock to jam after all these years in the vault cellar but to his astonishment, it sprang open as if it had been oiled only yesterday. Michael felt quite honored when he saw Padre José and Friar Hieronymus stepping aside to grant him the first view into the chest.

Michael was nervous, expecting the weapon to be in a miserable state after one hundred thirty years without being cleaned or oiled. The air in the bone chapel was quite humid, and Michael was sure that the gun must be heavily corroded by now. So, the young American prepared himself for a sad sight. Nonetheless, he was aware that he was about to see one of the most desired Colts in American history.

Friar Hieronymus carried the tall candle holder closer

to the prayer bench to grant Michael light for a better view. The first thing the expert for firearms saw was a red velvet lining. Surprisingly, the soft cloth had not suffered from the humidity in the cellar. It looked almost new. Michael shuddered when he realized the color reminded him of blood.

Bother José handed him a pair of cotton gloves. Michael wondered if the monk wanted to protect the relic or him. Gratefully, he put on the white gloves.

Michael's hands trembled slightly. After all the things they had discovered, he knew that Conway was in touch with evil, a fact that scared Michael. He carefully lifted the cloth with his fingertips and slowly folded it back over the rim of the box. The tension in the room was palpable, as if the spirits of the dead monks hovered over his shoulder.

Finally, he saw the Colt resting on the soft material and he gasped in shock. There she was! The weapon of evil. This was the very revolver which Josef Hernandez had named Arma de Diablo.

Michael couldn't help himself but had to admire the beautifully worked firearm. The colt was blued, and its serial number 222 was clearly visible, the engraving standing out as if it had been added only yesterday.

It was hard to believe but the six-shooter looked as if it had just left production. The metal shone like it had been polished a few hours ago. It seemed that the years passing had not harmed the weapon at all. The Colt 45 looked brand new, shimmering seductively as it sat atop the red velvet material. But how was that possible?

Michael carefully picked up the revolver. It felt lighter than expected and was extremely well balanced. He'd rarely held a weapon that was so precisely worked, fitting his hand perfectly. Ludwig Schmied had done an excellent job, considering the tools and machines for gunsmithing in those days.

"How in the world did he manage to build such a fine weapon," he whispered without looking at the other two men.

This revolver was the dream of every antique firearms expert. Suddenly Michael felt a tingling sensation at the tips of his fingers. The longer he studied the weapon the more fascinated he was.

"My hand is going numb," he whispered without realizing that he had spoken aloud. He didn't hear Friar Hieronymus talking to him, either. The young American was no longer aware of the two Benedictines or the bone chapel around him. He wasn't aware that his face showed a diabolic, cruel smile.

Fortunately, Padre José was familiar with the curse of the weapon, and he was not surprised that the spell affected Michael Kent. He always carried a rosary in the pocket of his cassock and quickly pulled it out to lay it across Michael's hand. The blessed cross made from silver dangled across the fingers of his American visitor.

The tingling sensation and numbness in his hand disappeared immediately. Instead, incoherent pictures crossed his mind. He whispered, "Oh my God, I see all the things that happened involving this gun. There's a cave, and Conway was there. He watched two men aiming guns at each other. A woman cries."

Michael shook his head as if to get rid of the frightening image. He grew paler as another deadly scene haunted his subconsciousness. Michael saw a man sitting on the ground besides a shallow creek. He placed the gun against his own temple.

"What do you see, my friend?" Padre José asked him.

Still holding the gun, Michael answered with a voice barely above a whisper, "A boy holds the gun and aims it at a drunk man. The boy and the man look similar to each other. God have mercy, he pulls the trigger."

Shaken, Michael dropped the gun back into the wooden casket. The visions stopped as quickly as they had appeared. He gazed down at the rosary across his hand, his heart pounding and his breath coming in short gasps. The Spanish monk nodded. He knew what Michael Kent had seen.

"It is true, all of it is true," a deeply shocked Michael whispered. "I have seen Conway in this vision. He was there, every single time that demon Conway was there. This gun is really cursed. God have mercy."

Michael looked down at the shimmering Colt 45, but his fascination for it had vanished. Instead, disgust and fear took over, and he felt sick to his stomach. His common sense wouldn't allow him to believe the story, but deep in his heart he knew the truth about the devastating Arma del Diablo. Knowing that there were many things that could not be explained with science books, he closed the lid of the trunk. Turning to Padre José and grabbing his arm, he whispered, "Bring me to your abbot, please. I urgently need his help."

It took over an hour, but finally Michael was able to meet the spiritual leader of Santo Domingo de Silos. He was surprised how young Abbot Anselmo looked. He seemed liberal-minded and greeted the Swiss Benedictine Hieronymus in Latin, obviously happy to see him. Then he shook Michael Kent's hand and introduced himself in English as Abbot Anselmo.

"Padre José told me what this visit is all about. I do have to admit that I was not at all prepared to come across a story that reminds me of the dark years of the Inquisition. Are you absolutely sure that this weapon carries this terrible curse?" Michael nodded but remained silent.

Abbot Anselmo studied Michael's pale face. Finally, he turned and walked to a huge desk made from a dark wood that dominated the entire office.

Abbot Anselmo picked up a leatherbound file of documents and returned to the three men waiting for him. He opened the folder and looked at them. "I have a document here which was originally kept in the private document collection of the very abbot who led this monastery during the time when Padre de la Vega returned from Santa Fe. It is written in Latin, but I will translate it to you, Mr. Kent: "And he created the tool of evil and belayed it with a terrible curse. From then on, every man who owns this tool of Beelzebub shall use it against his own flesh and blood or take his own life with it. God's heart shall suffer the same pain just as the Bringer of Light felt when his heavenly father chased him out of the Garden of Eden. The weapon that grants revenge for the shamefully treated son will carry its deadly spell until the very man who created the tool by the art of his own skills and hands can rob it of its deadly power. Only the one who once succeeded in expelling Satan shall be able to help break the curse. Beware of falling for the weapon's power, as it will destroy your own flesh and blood throughout centuries to come."

"Dios mío." Padre José whispered.

Friar Hieronymus's face looked ashen. "Good heavens, he describes Satan's eviction from Paradise, doesn't he?"

The abbot nodded, his face remaining serious. "I'm quite certain he does. When Padre de la Vega returned from the new world, he developed a high fever few days after arriving here at the monastery. His brothers feared for his life and were sure that he would not survive. He

was bothered by terrible hallucinations. As soon as he re-
gained consciousness, he asked for paper, ink, and quill.
He wrote down this prophecy. I admit, I thought of it as a
tale of yesteryear, and didn't believe the prophecy. May
God forgive me because now it looks as if de la Vega's
auguries have caught up with us. Now the question is, do
you, Mr. Kent, believe that you're capable of returning
the weapon to its creator where it is prophesied to lose its
power? Do you know where the mortal remains of that
gunsmith are buried? Do you believe it is possible to find
his grave after all these years?"

Michael repeated what the last surviving relative of
poor Ludwig Schmied had told him. He convinced the
leader of Santo Domingo De Silos that Ludwig's skeleton
was still buried in a family mausoleum in the blessed
earth of a cemetery in Connecticut. He also emphasized
that the mausoleum built on the sacred grounds of the
cemetery would most likely be untouchable for Mr.
Conway or whatever his name was. The firearms expert
was convinced that the revolver would lose its devilish
power once it was returned to the hands of the unfortunate
Ludwig Schmied.

"That collector who hired you—are you 100% sure
that he's the man in the drawing which de la Vega
brought from Santa Fe?"

Michael nodded in silence.

The abbot made the sign of the cross. He seemed extremely concerned and looked at the chest which Michael
had carefully placed onto the table in front of him. The
spiritual leader of Santo Domingo de Silos walked over
to his desk, picked up the phone and dialed a number
he had written on a piece of paper before the meeting
took place. He spoke to someone on the line in Spanish.

After a few minutes he hung up and turned to speak to the three men waiting for his next move.

"You should call this lady, what was her name? Frieda Miller, correct? Please inform her that the grave of her late relative, Ludwig, needs to be opened. I hope and pray that she agrees to that. The man I spoke to is a member of Opus Dei. His name is Ramon Hermando de la Riba. I assume that you have heard of Opus Dei, Mr. Kent?"

Michael nodded, feeling intimidated. Opus Dei was the strict Roman Catholic organization that followed direct orders of the Pope only. Rumors were that Opus Dei was a branch of the formerly feared Inquisition and private force of no one lesser than the Pope.

"I had already spoken to him before our meeting, and he asked me for a confirmation call in case our worst fears were proven true. Opus Dei has quite a bit of experience with cases similar to this one. You need to understand that such events were never made public by the Church—and for good reasons.

However, he fears for your safety if you take your originally booked flight back to the United States. Not only will people get suspicious if you carry a firearm in your luggage on a long-distance flight, but most likely Conway knows your flight dates as well. Under any circumstances we have to prevent the Colt from falling into the hands of Conway. Ramon Hermando de la Riba will accompany you back to the United States and make sure you arrive safely in Connecticut. You will be traveling under a different name and identity."

Astonished, Michael stared at abbot Anselmo. "How in the world will that work? We're not actors in some kind of James Bond movie."

"Please, Mr. Kent, don't ever underestimate the

power of the Mother Church. Unusual circumstances demand special actions, and we can provide them. You will depart with de la Riba the day after tomorrow. I suggest you try to rest a bit tomorrow and prepare yourself mentally for the task ahead, Mr. Kent. Ramon de la Riba is scheduled to arrive tomorrow evening. You will drive to Madrid together and take the oversea flight straight from there. Don't change or cancel your flight details. The travel agency of the Vatican will purchase a new ticket for you. In any case you cannot pass any information about new research results or the fact that you found that fateful gun to Mr. Conway. If you need to talk to him, try to keep him in the dark or even better delay revealing any facts as long as possible. You will be traveling incognito as a member of Opus Dei. Believe me, from now on you will be racing against time. Be our guest and prepare yourself for the mission ahead. May God protect and bless you, my son."

Friar Hieronymus, Padre José, and Michael left Anselmo's office and walked to the monastery's kitchen where a friendly nun served them hot café con leche.

"How do you feel, Michael?" Friar Hieronymus asked his American friend, who was unusually quiet.

"I'm truly afraid, and for the first time in my entire life, I fear the next day, Hieronymus. Besides, I'm not used to having others take the lead for me and tell me what I have to do."

He turned to Padre José and said, "Your abbot is used to giving orders like a general, isn't he?"

"Sometimes, whenever it's necessary. He's definitely not the kind of person that beats around the bush. However, you could still leave the revolver here in our monastery where it had been well-protected for one hundred thirty-six years," Padre José objected.

But Michael shook his head. "That is not possible. I'm afraid that I have let Gorgo Conway find your trail. He could hire someone else who would bring the Colt 45 to him like a puppy to his master. No, my dear friend, I have no other choice. Besides, I've promised his surviving relative Frieda to try my best to reinstate Ludwig's honor. After knowing everything about the events that took place in Connecticut, Ludwig doesn't carry the full blame for murdering his family members. I have high hopes that his soul might find peace if we succeed in breaking the spell of the six-shooter. There's no way I can undo the killings, but at least I can try to prevent history from repeating itself."

The three men separated after their conversation in the kitchen, and all of them withdrew to their rooms right after dinner. All were occupied with their own dark thoughts and none of them felt like engaging in small talk.

Michael couldn't believe that what seemed to be a harmless and lucrative job at first had developed into a dangerous, unpredictable adventure. Deep in his heart he knew that the story was true, but common sense made it difficult to accept.

***

The following evening Ramon Hermando de la Riba arrived at Santo Domingo de Silos. He introduced himself to the firearms expert. Michael immediately sensed that de la Riba was a tough, no-nonsense fellow. It was obvious that this man would not shy away from any danger.

De la Riba invited Michael into one of the small study rooms next to the library for a conversation. Michael filled him in with all the information he had gathered since his first meeting with Conway. When he finished his report, the priest of Opus Dei remained silent, his hands folded on the table. He studied the drawings and notes which Michael had laid on the antique desk. To his astonishment it seemed as if the Opus Dei member wasn't surprised at all. Father de la Riba had no doubts whatsoever about the entire story.

When the Spanish priest noticed Michael's puzzled expression, he looked him straight in the eye. "Mr. Kent, the Brotherhood of Opus Dei has studied the entire collection of documents from the dark times when the so-called Inquisition was active. I can assure you that not all reports about evil, Satan, or curses were invented or written down after torturing victims. Neither were they results of fake accusations. Much wrongdoing was going on those days, but apart from wild Hollywood fantasies, exorcism had been practiced for centuries for good reasons. And whether you believe it or not, we still have to conduct those rituals from time to time in different corners of this world."

Michael's eyes grew wide as he listened to the experiences of the priest.

"In our main archives in Rome, you would find documents that would leave you in fear for the rest of your life. I do not doubt at all that this pistol is cursed. We have to make sure we obtain access to the grave of that lamentable gunsmith. Therefore, I need to ask you to get in touch with his only surviving relative. It seems as if she trusts you. Furthermore, under no circumstances can any of this be told to Conway. We can't have him finding out that you're flying back to the U.S. tomorrow. The most important thing is that Conway doesn't discover that you actually found the gun and carry it on your flight back to the States. I have to ask you to turn off your mobile phone when we leave here tomorrow. That way we can ensure that your phone isn't being tracked."

Michael agreed to de la Riba's orders. The two men returned to their guest rooms. Michael packed up his belongings for the flight next morning. Abbot Anselmo handed over the chest holding the revolver to Ramon Hermando de la Riba. Most likely he was in the least danger from the spell of the Colt 45.

CHAPTER FOURTEEN

***

CEDAR HILL CEMETERY

The next morning Michael Kent, Friar Hieronymus, and de la Riba left the abbey of Santo Domingo de Silos after they bid farewell to Abbot Anselmo and all the other monks. Anselmo blessed Michael and wished him the best of luck.

At the airport Michael Kent had to say goodbye to Friar Hieronymus. He knew he would miss the educated monk. During his stay in Switzerland and Spain he grew very fond of Hieronymus. The man had deeply impressed him with his kindness and generosity. Michael promised his Swiss friend that he would visit him and his cousin, Brother Alexander in Switzerland again soon. He also invited him to pay a visit to beautiful Montana as soon as his house there was finished.

Finally, came the moment when he and de la Riba walked to the check-in counters in the international terminal which handled the flights to America. Michael was very worried that de la Riba might not be able to get the gun cleared through security. The weapon was packed inside the suitcase of the Opus Dei member.

The clergyman handed the additional documents, both passports, and two tickets to the young Spanish woman at the check-in counter. She seemed overwhelmed with the official Vatican documents which were unfamiliar to her, and she immediately called her supervisor. A trim man in his early fifties walked over to her counter and reviewed the documents she handed him. The man grabbed his walkie-talkie and fired off a few sentences in rapid Spanish. Then he returned the papers to the Spanish priest, ignoring the ground staff employee, and turned to talk to talk to the two passengers in front of the counter.

Since the airline supervisor was certain that Michael Kent couldn't understand Spanish, he addressed both men in English. "You are already checked in. Your luggage will be picked up by an airline representative and placed on the plane, and you will be accompanied personally through a different exit to your plane. The Vatican's Section for Relations with States informed me that you are transporting a precious relic. Therefore, we will scan your luggage separately under my personal supervision. Would you please be so kind as to follow me?"

Michael was speechless, but his travel companion didn't seem to be surprised at all. The American was developing an impression of the influence of the Roman Catholic Church in Europe. Hardly anybody in the U.S.A. would believe it if he told another American. However, the fact that they were supposed to leave their suitcases in the luggage terminal worried him. He hoped and prayed that both suitcases would make it into the cargo compartment of their plane.

He would have preferred to carry the revolver inside the wooden chest in his hand luggage. But of course, it was impossible to bring a firearm into the cabin of a plane. It was already astonishing that they were able to transport it in their suitcases without further difficulties or complicated paperwork.

After the shortened check-in procedure and scanning of their luggage, the two men walked over to a bar close to their departure gate. They enjoyed a strong coffee until their flight was ready for boarding.

"Are you sure that the chest with the Colt 45 is really safe in your suitcase?" Michael asked the man seated across from him.

"Oh, I'm quite certain. You know, it was no coincidence that the supervisor of the employee at the check-in counter took care of us so efficiently. His brother is a member of the clergy in Madrid, and he is in high hopes to be promoted to a position in Vatican City soon."

He winked at Michael and said, "We are all human beings, my dear friend. Even the men of the clergy are ambitious and keen to have a position in the center of power." The expert for firearms grinned.

Soon they were able to board the plane and take their seats. Wanting to appear like normal tourists, they flew economy and tried their best to make themselves comfortable in their seats. The expected flight time would be nine hours.

"Have you reached that lady in Texas to ask her if she would grant us permission to open the mausoleum?"

Michael nodded. "At first, she was astonished, or should I say shocked, but when she heard that there was a possibility of repairing poor Ludwig's honor, she didn't hesitate any longer and agreed to it. This morning she sent me an email to let me know that she'd already booked a flight to Connecticut and plans to meet us at Bradley

Airport. After that I turned off my mobile phone just as you asked me to."

Ramon nodded, obviously pleased. He turned his attention back to the newspaper which he had obtained from the flight attendant. The flight passed faster than Michael had feared, and they were able to go through immigration and customs processing without any difficulties.

While Michael tried to decide which hotel to book for their stay, his thoughts were interrupted by a cheerful, female voice calling him. "Michael, Michael Kent!"

Surprised he turned around and saw a happily waving Frieda walking briskly toward him. He introduced Ramon de la Riba who greeted her cordially.

She studied the Spanish priest's face for a moment but then took Michael's arm and asked him if he had booked a hotel already. Michael quizzically looked over to his Spanish travel companion who nodded.

"The 'company' booked three rooms for us. We will be staying in a hotel not far from Cedar Hill Cemetery." Michael laughed and Ramon grinned.

"Don't be surprised. I often refer to our organization as 'the company.'" Frieda stared from one to the other, obviously confused by their conversation.

Unlike Michael and Ramon, Frieda travelled with light hand luggage only. After retrieving the men's suitcases, they took a taxi, and Ramon told the cabbie the address of the hotel.

Once they had checked in, they searched for a restaurant close by. They asked for a table in a quiet corner somewhat distant from the other guests, and after ordering their beverages and food the two men told Frieda the reason for the visit in Connecticut and why they needed to open the family's mausoleum.

Both men had agreed to how much they would tell the elderly lady. Michael didn't want to scare Frieda. He had grown fond of her. Neither did he want to sound like a crazy person. It was a balancing act, but her strong Catholic faith helped them convince her of how important it was that the mysterious Colt was laid in Ludwig's coffin.

After finishing their dinner Frieda Miller leaned back in her chair and studied the faces of the two men sitting across from her. "Michael, you know that I built up a certain trust for you, and due to your position in the Opus Dei organization, I have to believe you as well, Signor de la Riba. Therefore, I give you permission to open the mausoleum and Ludwig's coffin, but I want you both to understand that this is the last thing I will allow anybody to do, even if the pope himself walked in here." De la Riba smiled warmly at that.

Frieda continued. "The fact that his secret chamber and his diary were found has caused enough turmoil and pain. I still believe that the past should be left alone. After all, the events were tragic and painful enough for my family. But in any case, I don't want to ruin the chance to grant Ludwig's soul some well-deserved peace. As far as I understand you, we might be able to erase the curse, and partly make up for murdering his relatives and his suicide."

"So, a walk to Cedar Hill Cemetery it will be tomorrow. However, gentlemen, it's time for this old lady to hit the sack now. Traveling here was tiring and it has been a long, tough day for me."

They took a taxi back to the hotel and each retreated to their own room.

The next morning, they met at breakfast, but somehow no lively conversation was possible. All three were nervous and withdrawn. They wanted to get the challenging task over with, so they headed out to the Cemetery before 10:00 a.m.

De la Riba carried the chest with the Colt 45 in a simple travel bag.

Both men left it up to Frieda to lead them to the grave site. She had a map of the cemetery and after searching for a while, they finally found the family's mausoleum. She opened her handbag and pulled out a big, antique-looking metal key. Michael had rather expected that they would need help from a cemetery employee, and his mouth dropped open.

Frieda laughed at his surprised face. "I'm his last surviving relative, remember? Therefore, I own a key which was shipped to me by the cemetery's administration."

She gave the key to Michael who walked toward the bronze door. The Opus Dei priest said a short prayer and made the sign of the cross.

The lock gave some resistance, and Michael had to be careful not to break the key. Finally, the corroded lock gave way, and the door open with a loud squeaking sound.

Stale air escaped with an angry hiss and the smell of dust tickled their nostrils. The firearm expert stepped respectfully aside and so did de la Riba. They wanted to grant Frieda the privilege of entering her family's crypt first.

Hesitating, she took a few steps inside the small chapel-like grave and looked at the four niches with the different coffins resting in them. On the right wall the two murdered men had found their place for eternity. On the left side two niches held the coffins of Ludwig's mother and the unlucky gunsmith. The only light filtered in through the open door.

Frieda carefully stepped toward the poor fellow's oak wood coffin and tenderly placed her hand on the lid. She bent her head and whispered a German prayer. Finally, she turned and motioned the two men to come forward while she stepped aside to give them space to move.

Both men crossed themselves before starting to work on the old hinges holding the coffin's lid. Michael hoped that none of the cemetery administrative staff would show up. He was fully aware that they committed an act of sacrilege.

After what seemed like endless minutes and with sweat appearing on both men's foreheads, the hinges yielded, and the coffin opened. Foul-smelling air escaped it. Frieda remained in the background. On the way to the cemetery, she had already proclaimed that she did not want to see the body. She found it rather distasteful to see what would become of her or her friends a hundred years from now. Michael understood her well as he wouldn't want to look into his relatives' coffins either.

De la Riba opened the cover, and they carefully leaned it against the wall of the niche. The priest said a short prayer and blessed the skeleton. Then he bent down and opened his travel bag, carefully pulling out the chest that held Ludwig's gun. He placed the box tenderly next to the coffin.

As Michael Kent waited for de la Riba's next move, the Spanish priest looked at him. "Do you remember the prophecy, Michael? 'The one who had succeeded in expelling the evil once must stop it again.' Archangel Michael against Satan, Michael Kent."

The man across de la Riba stared back at the priest, his stomach roiling with fear. Suddenly Michael felt a warm hand on his left arm. "Let's help Ludwig's poor soul, Michael."

Feeling Frieda next to him gave him the encouragement he needed to move. He nodded and pulled a pair of thick gloves from his jacket. After putting them on, he opened the wooden chest.

He carefully lifted the revolver from its red velvet cushion. The Colt 45 prototype shimmered seductively, and he could even see a reflection of himself. The grip of the gun seemed like polished onyx. He read the pistol's serial number as he held the gun and once again admired the craftmanship that had created such a precisely constructed, fine weapon.

He started to feel dizzy, and a tingling sensation spread through his fingers inside the glove. Michael closed his burning eyes for a moment. When he opened them again, he looked down at the serial number which now appeared blurry.

He blinked a couple of times, and, horrified, he watched as the numbers of the engraving changed right in front of his eyes. He could clearly read it now, and whispered, "My God, it is 666, the number of Satan."

The hand holding the Colt 45 trembled. Horrified, Michael realized that he was aiming at Frieda. Astonishingly, he had no control over what his hand did. The woman standing before him stared at him in disbelief.

As if from a distance, he heard the loud voice of de la Riba. "Holy Archangel Michael, stand by our side in this battle. Against evil and seduction by Satan you shall be our protection. May you send Lucifer and all the other evil demons who roam this world to poison our souls back to Hell where they belong. May you be blessed with the mercy and power of God. Amen."

The pistol in Michael's hand shook as he thought about Conway and young Josef Hernandez. He remembered Johnny Ringo and the unfortunate gunsmith Ludwig. With an outcry that reminded him of a wounded animal, he threw the revolver into the coffin where Ludwig's skeleton rested on faded linen. The numbness and tingling sensation in his hand stopped immediately, but he felt as if someone had sucked away the life energy from his body.

He leaned against the coffin, feeling weaker than ever before. Carefully glancing over the edge of the casket, he saw the Colt 45 laying atop the sternum, right where Ludwig's heart once hammered the rhythm of his short life.

Michael blinked a couple of times and thought his eyes played a trick on him. The gun was barely recognizable. The medal now seemed corroded and dull. The grip no longer looked polished, but rather porous and cracked as if it might fall apart any moment. It was almost impossible to read the serial number 222 since it was obscured with rust. The pistol looked as if it had rotted away in a humid old cellar for the past one hundred thirty years.

Ramon asked Michael, "Is it over?"

"I don't know for sure. I hope so. In any case, this six-shooter can no longer be used, considering the condition it's in now. It wouldn't function."

"Praise the Lord," the Spanish priest mumbled. Frieda stood behind the casket. She was very pale and whispered, "Rest in peace now, my dear Ludwig. May your sins be forgiven and may God welcome your poor soul."

The two men carefully closed the coffin, and Frieda gently caressed its lid once again. She whispered a German prayer. They turned and left the mausoleum. Michael closed the heavy bronze door and locked it. He placed the key into Frieda's outstretched hand.

Tears glistened in her eyes. "I thank you, Michael Kent."

They spent the rest of the day in silence, all three lost in their own thoughts. The events had taken their toll. On one hand, they were glad they were able to fulfill the prophecy, but on the other, they were aware that they had won only a small battle against evil which still held the world in its cruel grip.

The following day they all drove to the airport together. Michael and Ramon were both booked on the flight to Los Angeles, as the member of the Opus Dei organization intended to visit his friend, the Bishop of California. Frieda would fly straight back to San Antonio.

When the plane with the two men on board landed in California, Michael finally turned on his mobile phone. While still rolling along the runway, a text message from Gorgo Conway reached him.

> **What have you done, Michael? How can you betray me like this? You might have won a minor battle, but the war is not over yet, Michael Kent.**

He bent over to Ramon de la Riba and showed him the message. The priest nodded and said, "And that is the reason why Opus Dei will always remain active. Maybe you can join us one day. We could use a good `Archangel'." De la Riba smiled at Michael.

"I want to thank you Ramon. I would have never made it without you. The curse of the Colt almost got a grip on me."

***

They left the airport in Michael's car and drove through the wealthy suburb where Gorgo Conway lived. Ramon wanted to warn the archbishop and therefore intended to secretly take a few pictures of the house and, if possible, of the man known as Gorgo Conway.

When Michael drove toward the impressive villa, they immediately saw the sign of a well-known real estate company next to the driveway.

Puzzled, Michael left his car and saw a neighbor walking out of the garage next door. Michael waved at him and asked the man if Mr. Conway intended to sell his property.

"That weird fellow left already. A furniture van parked here, they packed couple of boxes and a few pieces of furniture and bang, he was gone. Just like that. He never talked with his neighbors, and I admit that I never liked him. Kind of an eerie fellow if you know what I mean. Even my dog, who is generally friendly to everybody, growled and barked whenever he saw him."

Ramon frowned. "Sooner or later, he will show up again in some corner of this world. Thanks to your research we know what he looks like, which means the fight continues. You are always welcome among us warriors, Michael. Think about it. I'm convinced that this is your destiny."

Michael dropped the clergyman off at the house of the archbishop and promised to stay in touch. A couple of days later he told his parents that he was returning to Montana for good and that he planned to build a house close to their home.

***

Two years later …

Michael continued to work as one of the most in-demand experts on antique firearms, but he had extended his expertise with additional studies and qualifications about religious relics.

He never told his parents why he had returned from California or why he had a sudden interest for artifacts collected by churches. His mother was convinced that it had to do with the visit in Maria Einsiedeln Abbey where his cousin Alexander lived.

She was aware that her son had changed. He attended church regularly and read the Bible quite often. Mrs. Kent sensed that something fundamental must have happened during his trip to Europe, but she never pushed him to tell her about it.

Michael Kent secretly joined the organization of Opus Die, working for them as a freelancer from time to time. Until his death many years later he admired and supported the Benedictines, and he never forgot Padre de la Vega. The Church won battles against Satan, but the war against evil will never end.

EPILOGUE

***

Three years after Michael Kent's death, an overweight man sat inside the cabin of a huge construction excavator. He had orders to prepare the place for the cement basement of a new shopping center.

His boss owned a well-known construction company. He was said to be very successful, unbelievably rich, and equally arrogant. The tabloid press pried into the business-man's life, but failed to learn his secrets as he kept out of public view and hardly ever appeared at society events.

The man was a myth. Nobody knew where he came from or how old he was. Members of high society wanted to be in touch with him and invited him to parties. Women tried to attract the attention of the charismatic man. But no one succeeded. He remained reclusive.

Peter had never liked that arrogant son-of-a-gun, but he needed this job. He envied the man for his wealth. Peter had to earn money like everyone else, especially after his ungrateful wife left him. She had ripped him off big-time and had taken the house as well as most of his bank account.

"That nasty witch has even bogarted my beloved RV. And my mendacious mother has helped her rob me. My own mother!"

Peter Greene felt the familiar hate and bitterness rising, and he cursed loudly in the cabin of the construction equipment. When he thought about the results of his costly divorce, his rage distracted him, and he thrust the shovel of the excavator much deeper into the ground than he meant to. A sudden jolt went through the vehicle as the shovel became stuck in the earth.

"Good grief, don't let that be a gas pipeline," he grumbled. Dang, that's all I needed today." To make things worse, he saw a fancy, black Mercedes limo turning the corner. His boss was about to make another unexpected visit to the construction site. "Great, that's all I need," Peter muttered under his breath.

Despite his big belly he jumped nimbly to the ground and walked to the front of the machine to get a better view of the shovel. Surprised, he realized he had unearthed a huge wooden trunk. Puzzled, he stared down at it. "What in the world is this? Maybe an old toolbox? But no, this is way too long."

The box was in sad condition and on the verge of falling apart. At once he understood and stepped back. "Almighty, isn't this the place where an old cemetery used to be? Butter my butt and call me a biscuit if this isn't an old casket. Wasn't there some scandal about the city council not relocating the graves and mausoleums according to the historic preservation society's order? I heard rumors that the property developers bribed the construction company to dig a big, deep hole and hide the ones that wouldn't fit at the new cemetery. What if word gets out they dumped caskets? They'll immediately stop construction, and I'll lose my job. Damn, what do I do now?"

"Is there a problem, Mr. Greene?" Peter Greene whirled around and stood face-to-face with the big boss himself, who he only recognized from pictures taken with telephoto lenses.

"No, Mr. Conway, no problem. I think my shovel got caught in something, and I just want to make sure I didn't damage a pipe or anything," Peter answered nervously. He always felt uneasy around the bosses. Contracting authorities were not his cup of tea.

"So, what blocks the excavator shovel?"

"My guess would be an old box or some wood, maybe tree roots" Greene answered, not meeting the man's piercing eyes.

"Well, let's take a look then, shall we?" the building speculator said softly.

After hesitating a moment longer, Peter Greene approached the rim of the excavation. "Damn it. There goes my job," he muttered angrily. The well-dressed businessman stood beside him, and to Peter's surprise a smile curled on his lips.

"I'll be darned. Looks like they re-buried some coffins down here. Don't you think so, Peter?"

Green blinked, dumbfounded. *Since when does he address me so cordially?* he thought. "Yes, sir, looks like it. My guess is that there's another one barely visible over there in the righthand corner of the hole."

"Hmm, I'd say your shovel broke through the casket right below us. That might cause some trouble for us."

Peter Greene nodded, lips pursed.

"Why don't you jump down there and peep through the hole to see if you can determine if the remains are still intact enough to be relocated? If so, we may have to call the dang city council." The man didn't look worried despite the possible trouble.

Peter carefully climbed into the pit. He saw that the shovel of his excavator had broken through the lid of the wooden casket. Disgusted, he wanted to turn away but obeyed his employer's orders. He stepped closer and peeked through the hole in the rotten wood, spotting the dull white of bones. Protruding between the sternum and the ribs of the skeleton, he saw an old revolver.

"Well, I'll be a monkey's uncle." The man removed his thick work glove and carefully slipped his hand through the hole in the coffin's lid. He grabbed the six-shooter and pulled it through the broken wood. The barrel and cylinder of the weapon were red with rust, and the tip of the hammer had flaked away. Only the ebony handle was still intact, though dull and dirty with age.

"Find anything besides old bones?" said the voice from above him.

Greene stared at the old gun. "An old six-shooter, sir. Now, who in this crazy world would want to be buried with a pistol? Looks like this fellow here wanted to defend himself even after he had bitten the dust."

"Bring it up so I can have a look at it." Greene scrambled out of the pit and stood breathless next to the man whose plan was to build the biggest shopping mall in the city.

"If you ask me, it ain't worth a nickel."

"Well, well, Peter, you never know. Beauty is in the eye of the beholder, they say." Peter Greene shrugged his shoulders. He couldn't see anything worthy about an old piece of junk.

"If you think about your wife, my friend, wasn't she the most beautiful girl in the world to you?" Greene stared at the man. What does his ex-wife have to do with this rotten six-shooter, and how would this guy know about his family affairs?

"She was beautiful to you, wasn't she? Until she showed her ugliness and true colors, didn't she?"

How in the world does he know about this? Am I the talk of the town after she ripped me off? Anger and bitterness rose like a burning flame.

"See, Peter, with this Colt it is rather the opposite. What looks ugly at first might turn into a real beauty."

Speechless, Greene stared at the Colt in Conway's hand. The seven-and-a-half-inch Colt 45 with its barrel shimmering blue as if it had been freshly polished now looked mighty tempting. The black material of the grip shone deeply. Its cylinder appeared to have been oiled only days ago, and he could now see a serial number engraved in the side of the weapon.

"Two, two, two," Peter read and smiled. But how is this possible? The gun he pulled from the coffin had been falling apart, buried with the body for God-knows-how-long. This one looked brand new.

He admired the revolver. He didn't know much about firearms, but he was quite sure that this one was a true antique and probably worth a nice amount.

"Want to hold it?" his superior asked temptingly. When Greene took the gun, the tips of his fingers started to tingle, and his hand gradually went numb.

"This fine weapon fits you perfectly, Peter. Makes you look like a strong, powerful man. What a shame that your ungrateful wife didn't appreciate you, and your own mother betrayed you so shamelessly. Maybe you should pay them both a visit with this fine Colt here. What do you say?" A grin split the man's face from ear to ear and his teeth glistened with saliva. But his eyes didn't smile.

Peter Greene nodded. He turned the gun over in his hand and walked to his car at the corner of the construction site. He left the excavator where it was with its shovel buried in the ground and keys still in the ignition.

The eerie-looking construction contractor Gorgo Conway turned around and walked slowly to his luxury limousine. He smiled and whispered, "Let the games begin!"

ACKNOWLEDGMENTS BY THE AUTHOR

***

The Colt 45 and Mr. Samuel Colt

The single action army Colt also known as a Peacemaker, Colt SAA, Colt 45, and Colt 1873 was the first cartridge revolver with a closed frame produced by Colt Firearms Manufacturing. Samuel Colt invented the basic parts of that legendary weapon while carving a model out of wood during a journey to India on a ship. At that time, he was no older than sixteen. His father sponsored two prototypes which unfortunately failed.

In 1836, Colt received the U.S. patent and began producing new prototypes. In 1845, the Texas Rangers ordered a large number of Colt revolvers, which luckily saved the company from bankruptcy. Samuel Colt developed his company further using a revolutionary mass production system and exchangeable parts long before Mr. Ford, the auto manufacturer, followed his example.

Samuel Colt died at only forty-seven years of age in his hometown Hartford, Connecticut. He is buried at **Cedar Hill Cemetery.**

The Colt Johnny Ringo used is an actual Colt SAA

caliber 45 with the serial number 222, which identifies it as a Colt of the early army order made in the first year of production. Therefore, it was not available for purchase by civilians. How Johnny Ringo came into possession of this particular six-shooter is unknown. After his death, it was sent to his sister and remained in the family for generations until the gun was sold to a collector in California. After that gentleman's death, it was auctioned to a private collector named Earle in 1980.

Johnny Ringo's Colt is one of the most valuable guns to have ever existed because its connection to a famous character of the Wild West heydays is thoroughly documented and proven.

Johnny Ringo

Most people know Johnny Ringo from Hollywood productions such as *Tombstone*. He was originally of West German/Dutch heritage.

He and his family travelled across the country with a wagon train, bound for California. His father shot himself accidently when he stepped off the wagon. Johnny Ringo was only fourteen when he witnessed it.

Ringo killed his first man when he was in his mid-twenties during the Mason County War in Texas. He was arrested but according to reports, acquitted. Rumor has it he escaped before being hanged and not actually acquitted.

After roaming the Arizona Territory, Ringo joined the gang of the Cochise County Cowboys and was said to have been involved in the assassination of Marshal Virgil Earp as well as the killing of his brother Morgan Earp. Seeking revenge, Wyatt Earp and Doc Holliday rounded up some friends and started a vendetta against the gang of cowboys, killing most of them.

On July 14, 1882, Ringo's body was found next to Turkey Creek. There was a bullet hole in his temple, and five rounds remained in his pistol. The death certificate stated suicide by self-inflicted gunshot wound, but people have always doubted it up to today. Neither the angle nor the position of the gun where it was caught in Ringo's watch chain matched the suicide theory.

Four men are suspected to have shot Johnny Ringo:

- Wyatt Earp, who claimed to have done so in some interviews, but denied it in others. Whether Ringo was a victim of Wyatt's vendetta is not known for sure.
- Doc Holliday, who had many reasons to shoot Ringo but was seven hundred miles away from Tombstone at the time of Ringo's death. Ringo had repeatedly called out Holliday during their days in Tombstone.
- Michael O'Rourke, who hated Ringo for leading a mob against him. O'Rourke had been blamed for killing a German miner. He was a gambler and never forgave Ringo for almost getting him lynched. Interestingly the man who saved O'Rourke from the mob was Wyatt Earp.
- Last, but not least, the famous Buckskin Frank Leslie, who told a guard at Yuma Territorial Prison that he shot Johnny Ringo. Interestingly, the fact that Billy Claiborne, another Tombstone Cowboys member, called Frank Leslie out for murdering Johnny Ringo. Frank Leslie shot Claiborne in the chest, but Claiborne repeatedly insisted on having seen Leslie shoot Ringo. Six hours after being shot, Claiborne died in Tombstone and is buried there.

Who really killed Johnny Ringo will remain one of the unsolved mysteries of the old West.

The Monastery of Maria Einsiedeln

The monastery of Einsiedeln was founded in 934 A.D. and dedicated to Holy Mary. The library is as old as the abbey itself and is often referred to as the mirror of spirituel life in Einsiedeln. At present the library contains over 230,000 printed books on every field of knowledge as well as 1280 handwritten books and over 1100 first print documents.

The historical books are stored in a hall which is a treasure of the baroque era. The monastery of Einsiedeln consists of one of the most beautiful baroque churches in Europe, as well as an elite college, a horse breeding stable, a modern sawmill, and a huge collection of arts and artifacts. Sadly, like most abbeys, Einsiedeln faces the same lack of younger monks deciding to live a life within the Benedictine Order.

Luckily, I am granted access to most parts of this outstanding abbey due to the fact that my cousin Alexander is one of the monks. He provided my inspiration for the character of Brother Alexander. Friar Hieronymus was a member of the Benedictine order for 75 years and died at the age of 97 in Einsiedeln.

Santo Domingo de Silos

The first monastery at today's Santo Domingo de Silos was founded 593 A.D. Unfortunately, Muslims destroyed it. Later, in 929 A.D. it was re-established as San Sebastian de Silos but was demolished a second time in 1002. The abbot Domingo de Silos built it up to today's glory and was its spiritual leader for over thirty years. After his death he was canonized as the patron Saint of the monastery, and its name was changed to Santo Domingo de Silos. In

December 1880, the order of the Benedictines took over the monastery and its library.

Their oldest document dates to 954 A.D. Santo Domingo De Silos is located in the province of Castille in north Spain and is open to visitors.

Cedar Hill Cemetery

Established in 1864, more than 32,000 people have been buried at Cedar Hill Cemetery. Encompassing 270 acres, Cedar Hill serves as an incomparable sanctuary for each of these people as well as for memorial artwork in Hartford history.

A private, nonprofit foundation helps to restore and to preserve historic memorials as well as care for the picturesque trees and plants. One of the famous people laid to rest there is firearms manufacturer Samuel Colt.

Archangel Michael

Archangel Michael is mentioned in different religions. In the New Testament Michael leads God's armies against Satan and his demons. He wins against Satan during a battle in heaven (Book of Revelation).

Archangel Michael was first worshipped as a healing angel in the fourth century. Over the course of time, he was seen more as a protector against evil and a leader of God's army.

He is mentioned in the Koran as well as in Judaism. Some Muslims believe that Archangel Michael was one of the three angels who visited Abraham.

People who follow Judaism believe that Michael was the advocate of Israel and helped to defend the Israelis against Satanael "the accuser," which stands for Satan.

Opus Dei

Originally founded in 1928, Opus Dei, which is associated with the Priestly Society of the Holy Cross, a Roman Catholic brotherhood that strictly follows the doctrines of the church. Opus Dei translates from Latin as "The Work of God."

Nowadays male and female academics, politicians, and scientists are welcomed members as well. In 2019 Opus Dei counted over 94,000 members worldwide. Originally founded to strengthen the position of the church within modern society, branches exist all over Europe. The leader of the organization is selected by the pope.

Members include well-known personalities from science, politics, sports, journalism, and of course high-ranking clergy members. Opus Dei is the most influential organization inside the Vatican.

Since the members try to keep their activities hidden from the public, only a little is known about Opus Dei. The rumor that Opus Dei is a successor of the Catholic Inquisition was never proven.

Ramon Hermando de la Riba was indeed a priest and member of Opus Dei.

Credits:

This book wouldn't have been possible without the following people:

My beloved cousin Brother Alexander and all the monks from Maria Einsiedeln, who always welcome me with open arms, spiritual guidance, and access to the amazing library.

Pam Van Allen, my language consultant, who always advises me when it comes to the use of the English language. It is a true pleasure to work with her on my books. This is even more true since she is a valuable friend now.

The amazing team from Wolfpack Publishing. I am honored to run with the pack.

Western historian, author, and actor in well-known movies such as "Tombstone," Mr. Peter Sherayko, who supported me with important facts about Johnny Ringo's gun. I am proud to call you a friend, Peter!

TAKE A LOOK AT, THE UNFORGIVING DAUGHTER

***

CAN YOU ALWAYS TRUST THE MEN WHO RIDE BY YOUR SIDE?

Standing by the grave of her murdered father, Sheriff Townsend, Elli swears she will bring justice upon the killers. Unfortunately, the only man who can help her is about to be hung for a crime he did not commit.

Elli must free Armando Phillipe Diaz to defeat the outlaw pack led by the ruthless Texas Logan. A dangerous chase leads to a long-lost treasure and into a deadly trap. Will Elli Townsend survive and be able to fulfill her oath to her father?

"If you like your westerns sprinkled with gunplay, revenge, romance and unlikely allies; this is the book for you." – Rod Timanus

ON AMAZON NOW

ABOUT THE AUTHOR

***

As someone born and raised in Germany, author Manuela Schneider's love of American Native and Western history might be surprising to some. But her fascination with pioneer life, cowboy heroes, and treacherous outlaws have been her constant companion for as long as she can remember.

As a child, Schneider recalls being mesmerized by American TV shows like Gun Smoke, Little House on the Prairie and Bonanza. In her adult years, Schneider fueled her deep interest in the American West by traveling to the U.S.A. and visiting historic sites like Tombstone, Monument Valley, and Kanab, UT. After experiencing the wild beauty of the Southwest first hand, her desire to write stories of love, struggle, and survival in the Wild, Wild West became even stronger.

After leaving a successful career designing motorcycle fashion for the European market, Schneider penned her first Western fiction novel in 2017.

When not researching or penning riveting stories about Western boomtowns and Native American life, Schneider can be found traveling all over the world, enjoying silver jewelry and spur smithing, studying archaeology as a hobby, and writing her own Western travel blog on manuelaschneider.com.

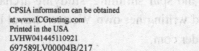

9 781647 347451